A NOVEL

PITBULLS
IN A
SKIRT 2

MIKAL MALONE

CARTEL PUBLICATIONS
PRESENTS

PUBLISHER'S NOTE:
This book is a work of fiction. Names, characters, businesses, organizations, places, events and incidents are the product of the author's imagination or are used fictionally. Any resemblance of actual persons, living or dead, events, or locales is entirely coincidental.

Library of Congress Control Number: 2009922312
ISBN: 0-9794931-9-6
ISBN 13: 978-0-9794931-9-5
Cover Design: Davida Baldwin www.oddballdsgn.com
Editor: Right Way Editorial Services
Graphics: Davida Baldwin
www.thecartelpublications.com

First Edition

Printed in the United States of America

DEDICATION

This is dedicated to all the fans of Pitbulls In A Skirt.

I hope I did you proud.

ACKNOWLEDGMENTS

To everyone who has ever picked up my book and <u>got it</u>, this novel is for you.

What's Good Babies,

It feels great to introduce Pitbulls In A Skirt 2 and we're sure you'll love it. A lot of energy went into bringing these characters back in a way you've never seen them before. We know you'll appreciate how these women have grown and the challenges being bosses bring to them.

On another note, so much has happened since our first year in business. We are blessed to be experiencing the success we have and we're eternally grateful. As always, we must pay homage to an author who's paved the way. With that said, we'd like to show love to:

Anna J"

Anna is a trailblazer author of our time. Her novels, *My Woman His Wife, The Aftermath, Get Money Chicks* and *My Little Secret* have caused quite a stir within the urban industry. Anna knows how to grab her readers and keep their attention! Anna keep penning the fire hits! We love what you do!

Stay Smart, Sexy and Strong!

T. Styles
President & CEO, The Cartel Publications
www.thecartelpublications.com
www.myspace.com/toystyles
Email: tstyles@thecartelpublications.com

PROLOGUE

Aleed's black Nike boots pressed against the grungy snow as he ran for his freedom. Having six warrants out for his arrest and a pocket full of crack rocks, he knew he'd be going down for a long time if the persistent cop caught him.

"Freeze! Stop running before I shoot!" the young-black-rookie cop yelled.

His loyalty to his job impacted his decisions. All he wanted was Aleed, the man whose picture was pinned against the police station wall he saw everyday.

"If you don't freeze...I'm gonna fuckin' shoot! I'm not playin' wit you!" the cop taunted. "Stop runnin'!"

When Aleed saw the green awning over the gate in Emerald City, he felt a sense of calm. He knew that once he got over the gate, the rules the outside world lived by would not apply.

"This is my final warning," the cop yelled as they ran down the dark sidewalk a few feet from the level of the fence. Aleed leaped over the fence.

And then the cop heard Aleed yell, "Ecilop! Ecilop!"

The cop thought the yell was weird but remained on his trail. He didn't realize that "Ecilop" stood for police backward. It was the code word for Emerald city to lock down shop and get out of dodge.

Instead of hopping the fence like Aleed, he ran through the entrance gate, past the empty guard's station and onto Emerald's grounds. Once inside, he noticed that

Emerald appeared vacant. As always the five buildings of Emerald City encompassed a large yard in the middle. It was pitch dark and no lights were on not even in the yard. Emerald City was in order.

"Aleed, get out here! Don't make things worse!" his voice echoed and bounced back to him off the buildings. "Aleed! I know you hear me!"

The gun he was holding shook in his hand and the darkness and silence frightened him.

Then he heard, "What you doin' here cop? What you doin' on E.C. grounds?"

The officer heard the voice and it appeared to come from the top of one of the buildings but he couldn't see the man or his face.

"I'm a police officer and I'm here for Aleed."

"Well if you a D.C. cop you should know your laws don't apply here. Leave now...while you still can." The man's disregard to his shield enraged the rookie cop.

"I'm not goin' nowhere without Aleed! I'm the mothafuckin' law!"

The person laughed and others laughed behind him, their voices hidden within the night.

"Check dis out, COP ...right now, the choice is yours to leave. But when I count to three, the choice will be yours no more. We run fuckin' Emerald City and everybody in it!" He yelled to the top of his lungs sending chills through the cop's tender heart.

"One!" the voice began.

"I'm a police officer!" the rookie yelled backing up cautiously.

"Two!" was followed by a clicking sound of many weapons upon the rooftops.

"You can't get away with this!" the officer continued.

But before he could say, three, the cop was gone. With his life in tote.

WELCOME TO EMERALD CITY!

MERCEDES

"WE MAKE THIS SHIT LOOK EASY."

I can't believe I'm runnin' late! I am dodging in and out of traffic trying to make it to Emerald city on time. I should not have been fuckin' wit' Derrick's sexy ass this morning. That man must've fucked me in every room in our loft style apartment at DC's National Harbor. Lifting up slightly, I tug at the seat of my Seven jeans between my legs. They were rubbing against my pussy causing me discomfort, but damn does that boy have some good dick. It's a good thing my kids were with their father because I'm not sure if I would've been able to keep my voice down.

I thought I knew what love was when I was with Cameron. I couldn't see the sun or the moon unless Cameron was with me. It's amazing what separation and a near death experience can do for a relationship. Bottom line is this, now that I've been in Derrick's presence, I know what real love is and I'm not willing to trade it for any man in the world…not even for Cameron.

When I pull up to the Emerald City gate, I am immediately transformed. No longer am I a girlfriend or a mother. In Emerald City, I'm a boss! Glancing at the five buildings with green awnings circling the open field, I respect its power.

"Good morning, ma'am," says the security guard at the gate. "The other ladies just got here. They're in the field."

"Thanks, Jake. How's the baby?"

"Growing bigger everyday," he smiles. "He'll be two tomorrow."

"That's right! It *is* his birthday."

"Yes, ma'am, it is."

"Well you can have the day off to spend with your family. I'll get Amir to guard the gate for you."

"Thanks, boss! I appreciate it!" I wait until the gates open and drive my new black Mercedes Benz G-Class truck inside.

Once inside, I see my girls standing outside with their cars surrounding them. Although cold outside, the sky is icy blue. As usual they're draped in fur coats and diamonds and I can't help but smile. We were the fly-est drug bosses in DC, hands down! We make this shit look easy. Yvette's red Lincoln Navigator is parked next to Kenyetta's silver Lexus LS and I pull up next to Carissa's blue Porsche. I can't wait to get out of my ride and hug my friends.

"About time you got here, bitch!" Yvette yells, as my girls' crowd around.

"Shut your short ass up! Better late than never."

"No…your ass always late!" Carissa interjects.

"What is this…shorties gang up Mercedes day?" I laugh. "Kenyetta you got my back right?"

"You know it," she smiles.

We embrace one another. Ever since we made a decision to move out of Emerald and run our operation from the outside, we saw each other less. We talked as much as we could, but we had our own lives. No matter what, we agreed to return and spend a week in Emerald City each month and no one knew but us which week we'd choose. We did this to remain spontaneous and leave nothing to chance.

I glance on the rooftops and see our shooters in place. Whenever we were in Emerald, security was tighter than security protecting the president.

"Fuck all that bullshit, look at that truck!" Yvette says. She traded her short spiky hair for a cute shoulder length bob. "When you get that? And what happened to the car?"

"I still got my car and if you would answer your phone sometimes, you woulda known I got this last Friday," I tell her examining the black waist length fur coat she wore with her jeans and black Gucci boots.

"Oh here we go again," she says, brushing me off. "Like you always answer your phone."

"She's tellin' the truth, Yvette. You ain't the same. Everything good with you?" Carissa questions as she tries to close her full length chocolate coat tighter. The wind was blowing harder.

"Don't start with me because we all have personal lives, including me."

"Yvette we're still family and family keeps in contact. So you tell us, how are things really going with you?" Kenyetta asks. I notice her eyes seem sad. "You ain't got no kids or no man so what's up with you?"

Yvette looks at all of us and drops her head before brushing her hair out of her face. I feel bad for putting her on the spot but I care about her. I care about all of them. Just because we leave Emerald doesn't mean that changes. We worth fuckin' millions! Niggas would love to kidnap one of us just to make some cash. We have to watch each other's backs.

"What's up, Vette?" I persist.

"Can we just leave it alone, Mercedes? I just need to get into my apartment, grab a drink and relax. It's cold out here."

"Why you in a rush to go into that lonely ass apartment anyway?" Carissa asks beating her feet for warmth.

"Yeah, bitch!" I tell her, looping my arm through hers. "You do seem a little anxious. You sure you ain't gettin' high on our supply?"

"I'ma fuck you up, Mercedes!" she laughs. "I'ma do better about calling when we away from Emerald. And ya'll betta take that because it's all I can give right now. So can we please get out of this cold air and go inside? Carissa sound like she in a marchin' band or somethin'."

"Aight, bossy," I tell her. "I'ma let you off the hook for now, but you gonna tell me what's up with you."

"Yeah...and if you do have a man we want to meet him," Carissa adds. "I gotta tell his ass however many times he fuckin' you, he betta increase that shit by three because you wound up!" We all laugh.

"Trust me, I'm gettin' sexed more than all of ya'll put together. I guarantee that."

"Doubt it!" I laugh.

"That's real talk! Way more!"

"Oh really...," Kenyetta says. "I guess we better get inside our apartments, drop our shit off and finish this meeting so we can hear the juicy details."

We chit chat a little longer and jump in our rides. As I pull off, I can't help but think about Yvette again. Something is definitely up.

YVETTE

"I LOVE WHEN WE HAVE DRUNK SEX."

I'm in love! And I didn't think it would be possible after Thick died. I felt dead inside before her and all I wanted to do was see her face again.

I open the apartment door and smile when I smell the scent of fried chicken, cheese rice and broccoli simmering on the stove. My girlfriend Chris, or C. Wash as she likes to be called, spoils me to death.

Although the relationship has its high times, it's not easy being gay. The stares from people and the comments from men who see us walking in public mess my head up sometimes. But when we're alone, nothing else seems to matter.

I still remember the first day I saw her face.

◄┄┄►

ABOUT 2 YEARS EARLIER

Yvette was driving down Benning Road in the Northeast section of D.C. headed toward Agatha's, an old friend of her mother's, house. Agatha cared for Yvette's darkest secret, her strung out mother. No one knew except Thick, who Yvette killed a few weeks earlier that her mother was even alive.

Loretta was so strung out that she couldn't care for Yvette and her two sisters. Loretta was a horrible mother. She proved it when she left Andrea, a baby, in laundry room during one of DC's worst winter storms . She died a few hours later. It was also Loretta who pulled over on the side of a dark road somewhere in Virginia, to put her other

-6-

daughter Cecil out because she couldn't afford to feed her drug habit and both of her children. So she made a choice to nurture her broken veins. To this day Yvette didn't know if her sister was dead or alive.

As a child, Yvette often had to lay in strange beds with her mother while she had sex for money. She still remembered how they tried to pry their fingers into her virgin womb because sleeping with Loretta was too atrocious by itself.

So when Yvette got old enough to understand that sex paid, she left the small bathroom she lived in with her mother for six years and headed to Emerald City. She couldn't wait to leave the filthy conditions her mother's pimp subjected them to in his four bedroom home.

The first day she arrived in Emerald, she hopped off the bus with all of her possessions in a blue torn backpack. It was a summer night and the tight blue jean shorts and white t-shirt she wore hugged her curves, exuding more sex appeal than a young girl should have. Off the bus for two minutes, her first trick pulled up next to her in a shiny blue Suburban and she was immediately attracted to him.

"You wanna take a ride with me?" he asked eyeing her huge breasts. "You don't look like you old enough to be out here by yourself."

Yvette, nervous at the man's huge and powerful persona said, "Okay."

"What's your name, shawty?" he questioned when she got inside.

"Yvette."

"I'm, Thick," he said in a voice that made Yvette's virgin body shiver.

"Thick," she giggled. "I like that."

"If you like that, I got somethin' else you'll love. I'll tell you *all* about it."

Thick, who was twenty one at the time, took a sixteen year old Yvette into his apartment in Emerald and molded her sexually and mentally. She couldn't eat, sleep or breathe unless he told her to. And if she showed emotion, he'd beat her.

Over time the only problem he had with Yvette was her lack of cleanliness. She didn't know how to clean because her mother lived a filthy lifestyle. After awhile, Thick dealt with the problem by never being home.

A year later, Loretta showed up on their doorstep needing help and Yvette almost fainted. She heard from drug dealers where Yvette lived and tried to extort money from them. But when Thick refused, she threatened to tell the police that he was molesting her underage daughter. Thick told Yvette to get her mother away before he placed what was left of her wretched body six feet deep. He also promised to put her out.

Yvette who discovered a new life in Emerald, friends and a man, didn't want to leave the only family she'd grown to love. It took Yvette five hours to find her drug addicted mother a home. That's where Agatha came in. For five hundred dollars, she provided a roof for Loretta and maintained Yvette's secret by not letting anyone know that her mother was alive.

And now many years later Yvette was bailing her mother out of trouble again.

"Agatha, I'm pulling up now," Yvette said on the phone.

"Well you gotta hurry up! This bitch has gone too far this time!"

"Agatha, calm down. I'm coming," Yvette said growing impatient.

"You said that two hours ago! This bitch done tried to shoot up through a vein in her eye 'cause the ones in her arm so fucked up! Now I know you got that good job at the phone company, so you should be fine finding her somewhere else to live. But she gotta leave here today!"

Yvette took a deep breath and pulled up to Agatha's house. She never told her she sold drugs because she didn't want her asking for more money. For that reason, she told her that she was employed with the phone company. And since most employees were paid well working there, she bought her story.

"I'm here."

"Good...she gonna be outside! Bye."

Yvette got out of her car right before her mother was thrown out front wearing nothing but a blue nightgown. Loretta's once smooth chocolate skin was now as dark as charcoal and uneven. Her body was frail and she looked older than her true age. Yvette desperately tried to rid herself of the pity she felt seeing her mother's horrible condition.

"Where am I gonna take you?" she said to herself as she walked up the five steps.

She couldn't even call on her friends for help because they didn't know about her.

"Loretta, can you walk?" Yvette asked.

She was lying against the door with her legs wide open exposing her naked vagina. Yvette looked around to see if anyone was looking and everyone was.

"Loretta. Come on," Yvette said as she helped her mother up. She was as short as Yvette.

They almost fell down twice because Loretta was off balance. When Loretta almost caused Yvette to fall, she released her and watched her topple down two steps and hit the ground.

"Fuck! What am I gonna do wit you! Why do you have to be a washed up ass addict? Why couldn't I have a mother who cares for me? I hate you!" Yvette cried as she stood over her.

PITBULLS IN A SKIRT 2

As she yelled at her mother, she saw a black Lexus pull up in front of the house and park.

"Fuck you doin', young?" Seven, Chris's sister asked when they parked. Seven's tiny neat braids dressed her head. Although everything about her mannerisms resembled a boy, she was extremely pretty and possessed a smooth brown complexion. "You know we gotta get to the Terrace and pick up that stack."

"Slim, we up the street, fall back. We gonna get there," Chris said placing her hazard lights on.

"Oh...I see what you doin," Seven said looking at the short girl with big titties trying to pull another woman inside a car. "Always chasin' bitches."

"Shut your dyke ass up!" Chris said exiting the car. "I be right back."

When Chris got out, she walked up to Yvette who was struggling to put her mother inside her white Infiniti.

"You need help with your folks?" Chris asked walking up to Yvette from behind.

"No! I got it myself."

When Yvette finally looked at Chris, her heart skipped a few beats. The tall girl with light brown eyes made her melt. She'd never looked at another woman sexually but was attracted to Chris instantly. Her vanilla complexion and neat row braids added charm to her persona.

"You sure?" Chris lifted her mother up anyway, and with one scoop, placed her inside the car. "You look like you strugglin', sweetheart."

When Loretta was inside, Chris looked at Yvette and caught her smiling at her.

"You aight, cutie?" Chris asked.

"Oh...uh...yes, I'm fine."

"You sure? Cuz you look out of it."

"I'm...I'm...fine."

"Cool...so what's your name?"

"Why?! I'm not gay!" she yelled realizing quickly how ridiculous she sounded.

"Whoa!" Chris said with her hands extended in front of her. "All I asked was your name, ma. I wasn't tryin' to get wit' you."

"Oh."

"Not yet anyway," Chris winked. Yvette didn't respond. "So what's your name? You do have one don't you?" she smiled.

"Oh...yes, I'm sorry. Yvette. My name's Yvette."

"Aight, Yvette, where you takin' her?"

"Why?"

"Cuz I know somebody who might be able to help you get her together. My aunt went there a few years ago and she been clean ever since. Now she work there. It's a small place in Baltimore that not a lot of people know about. The joint kinda illegal, but it works." Chris took her Blackberry off of her hip and scrolled through her contact list. "The number is 4...1...0...," she stopped when she saw Yvette wasn't recording the number. "You gotta phone?"

"Yes," Yvette said still caught off guard by her attraction to Chris. "I'm ready."

"Look, why don't we do this. You take my number, and when you get a chance give me a call. I'll tell you more about the spot. That way you can make sure it's the right place for your peoples. Cool?" Before she could respond Seven laid into the horn like she'd lost her mind.

"Slim, are you serious?! I'm comin'" Chris yelled.

"Well hurry the fuck up den, nigga!" Chris ignored her. "Call me anytime, Yvette. I mean that. And don't worry...I know shit seem fucked up right now, but they'll get better. You too pretty to be frownin'."

When Chris walked off, Yvette didn't leave her position until Chris was out of sight. She couldn't describe the feeling she felt around her. She'd felt that feeling one other time in her life and that was with Thick.

Yvette took her mother to the rehab center and two large men came and took Loretta away. Yvette didn't mind taking a chance with an illegal facility because the last time she placed her mother in a traditional rehab; she made a crawl space under the wired fence and ripped the skin on her back to shreds trying to escape.

After leaving rehab, Yvette and Chris hung. What started out being days together ended up being months. And before long, they purchased a luxury apartment in Georgetown DC. They'd been together ever since.

◄┈┈┈►

PRESENT TIME

"There go my, bitch," Chris says as she pushed me up against the door and giving me an extra wet kiss. I taste the liquor on her breath and I am aroused. I love when we have drunk sex. "Why you keep me waitin' so long, Vette?"

Before I answer she takes off my coat and flings it to the floor. Once my jeans are down she runs her warm tongue in and out of my wet pussy. I bite my bottom lip to prevent my neighbors from hearing our dirty little secret. It doesn't take long before my love oil eases out of my body. She's a pro.

"You are a trip," I say trying to regain my composure as I pull up my jeans.

She doesn't respond...she just straightens her clothes and dishes our plates. Placing the dishes on the new table she says, "What are you looking at?"

"What you think I'm looking at?"

"I don't know but if you keep staring like that, I'ma find out."

"I tapped out a long time ago," I tell her trying to come down off of my sexual high. "You are too much for me."

"Don't say stuff you don't mean," she winks.

We are eating at the table when she says, "So was today the day?"

My stomach flips and I try to act like I don't know what she's talking about even though I do.

"What you talkin' about, Chris?" I ask looking up from my meal.

"You know what I'm talkin' 'bout. When you goin' tell your friends 'bout us? When you goin' stop playin' games and let them know we together?" her fork drops in her plate and she sits back in her chair.

"I will, Chris. But you can't rush me."

"We been fuckin' wit' each other almost two years now. And they still don't know 'bout me. So how is that rushin' you?"

"Chris, please!" I say getting up from the table. I stand in front of the window and look down at our empire. For a brief moment, I question my sexuality and my life. "As long as you keep eatin' this pussy right…we good."

"Who you talkin' to like that?" she asks walking up to me.

In life I'm known as the hardcore bitch. And don't get it twisted, I still am, but there's something about Chris I respect and at times I find myself backing down.

"I'm sorry, baby," I say turning around to face her. "I'm just frustrated. My love for you should be enough."

"That's not it," she says rubbing my shoulders. "I'm tired of being a secret, Yvette. I'm ready to be a part of your *whole* life."

I look into her brown eyes and feel sad about my embarrassment of our relationship.

"I'll tell them this week."

"For real?!" She asks and her eyes widen.

"For real," I say kissing her lips. "I'll tell them before we leave Emerald." I can smell my sweet love juice on her mouth and get aroused again. "But right now," I continue walking her to the dining room chair. "Let me return the favor you gave me earlier."

As I pull down her jeans, move her boxer briefs to the side and lick her wetness, my stomach flutters. Who knew I'd take pleasure in being with a woman. I don't know how I ended up here, but here is where I belong.

KENYETTA

"WHATEVER YOU NEED ME TO BE I WILL BE."

I had an hour to meet my friends at the community center inside of Emerald City. We had a lot to discuss about our day to day operations. But before doing anything, I jumped back into my car and took a drive a few blocks down to Tyland Towers to see BW. I know it's fucked up of me to be dealing with a competitor, but it is what it is. You can't help who you love now can you? Anyway, he said he had something important to talk to me about tomorrow but I can't wait. I have to know now! This roller coaster relationship is killing me! At times I wish he wasn't in my life, but I'm in too deep and can't turn back now.

◀ ⋯⋯⋯⋯⋯⋯⋯⋯⋯⋯⋯⋯⋯⋯⋯⋯⋯⋯⋯⋯⋯⋯⋯⋯⋯ ▶

1 YEAR EARLIER

"Sir, I'm tryin' to be nice but you're making it hard. Where is my car?" Kenyetta asked the salesperson at the counter in Sparkles detail shop.

"What kind of car you got again?" the overweight man responded, the tip of his nails black with oil and soot.

"The red Volvo with the tinted windows."

"Oh yeah," he said looking through a few sheets of paper on a worn out clipboard. "You got one more person in front of you and then you should be good."

"One more person in front of me? But I was the first one here this morning."

"Like I said you got one more person in front of you," he said angrily without regard for her feelings. "Wait or get your car the fuck out of here!"

Kenyetta threw her weight in the grungy orange plastic seat and tried to prevent the tears from escaping her eyes. Dyson's funeral was in an hour and it didn't look like she was going to make it. She found out about it days earlier and although they weren't together, she couldn't wrap her mind around him being gone. The news came to her suddenly while on the steps of Unit C.

"Hey, Yvette," Aleed said, walking up to her. "I don't know if ya'll know yet, but somebody killed Dyson."

"What?" Yvette said. "Who told you that?"

"Everybody's talkin' about it," he said slowly looking at Kenyetta. "I just thought ya'll should know." When Aleed left they looked at Kenyetta with concern.

"I'm fine," she told them before they asked. "It ain't like we were together or nothin'. It's been over between us."

Kenyetta tried to keep her head up, but when she left their sight she cried herself to sleep. She didn't bother telling them she was going to the funeral. She wanted the last moments she'd spend with Dyson to be alone. And now here she was, stuck in the detail shop, wondering if that moment would ever happen.

While sitting in her seat pouting, the door to the shop flung open. An extremely tall and stocky man walked in wearing blue jeans, butter colored timberlands and a black leather coat. His skin was dark and his hair was neatly cut. He had swag and build like Biggie did when he had money. A white hand towel rested on his shoulder and he wiped the sweat off of his head with it periodically. Although Dyson was considered more attractive, the stranger still had sex appeal.

"My ride ready, playa?" he asked the man at the counter.

"You know we got you. Give me a second." Seeing this, Kenyetta stood up and walked hurriedly to the counter.

"Hold up, why is his car ready before mine?"

"He was here before you."

"Bullshit! I'm sick of you!"

"You know what...I'm tired of your shit too," the sales person barked. "Take your car and get the hell out of my shop!"

He flung the keys to Kenyetta and she snatched them off the counter and said, "You betta hope I get over this by the time I get to my car because you don't know who you fuckin' wit'."

Kenyetta pushed the glass door open and stormed outside. Without asking, she stormed in the back disregarding everyone who was working there to get her car. Five men who were inside moved out of the way of the line of her rage.

"Can I help you?" one of them asked.

"Get the fuck out my face. You don't know me!" She jumped inside of her car and was preparing to pull off when Black Water blocked her path.

"Excuse me?!" she yelled outside of her driver's window. "You betta get out of my way before I run your ass ova!"

"You not gonna do that," he smiled. His teeth were white and she loved his smile.

"I'm serious. I'm not in a good mood."

"Why don't you get out and talk to me for a second?"

Kenyetta exited her ride and walked up to him. Although she was 5'7, he had almost a foot over her with her heels.

"What is your problem?" she asked with her hand on her hip and her Louis Vuitton purse on her shoulder.

"Calm down, ma. You too pretty to be so mad."

"There's no such thing," she corrected him. "And I'm tired of niggas tellin' me I'm too pretty to do this…and I'm too pretty to do that!"

"Maybe you tired of hearing it because it's true."

"No! What I'm tired of is being taken advantage of because of the way I look. All I wanted was to get my car washed and it's obvious that's not happening."

"Hey, get that car done in ten minutes and I'll pay ya'll double," Black said ignoring her momentarily. She turned around and saw all men stopping their conversation, to tend to her car.

"What's goin' on?"

"What you think goin' on? They cleanin' your ride."

"I'm not payin' these mothafucka's shit! I been in here all day!"

"Don't worry 'bout that. They goin' take care of you and then you'll be free to go wherever you goin'. Cool?"

Kenyetta immediately took comfort in his take control kind of personality. He reminded her of Dyson in that way.

"You know what, right now, I don't even care," she told him.

"So where you goin', Kenyetta?"

Because she hadn't told him her name, she became defensive thinking this was a set up.

"How you know my name?" she asked sticking her hand in her purse, touching her weapon. She wouldn't hesitate putting a bullet through his face if she had to. "I didn't tell you my name!"

"Calm down. I saw your name on the sign in sheet inside the shop," he saw her remove her hand from her bag.

"Why you so uptight? You involved in some illegal shit or somethin'?"

"No...uh....why you say that?"

"Cause that's how you actin' diggin' in your purse and shit. What you got in that bag, ma?" She didn't respond. "You real hostile."

"I know," she laughed softly. "And I'm sorry about my attitude. It's been a long morning and I have a lot to do."

"Let me help clear your mind," he said taking a few strands of her hair into his hand without asking. "I love black women with silky hair like this."

"You awfully touchy feely," she said moving her head so that her hair escaped his grip.

"Naw, I just go after what I want."

"And what you want is me?" she sounded more hopeful than she wanted to.

"I like what I like," he said towering over her. "I also know if you got a man, he 'bout to not exist."

His comment brought her back to reality and she remembered Dyson's funeral. Although they weren't together when he was murdered, he was the last man she had.

"Uh...listen, I'm sorry but I have to leave."

"What you late for a funeral or somethin'?"

"I have to go," she repeated avoiding his comment. She smiled when she saw her car was done. "I'll pay you back for this."

"I'm sure you will. And I got your number from Sam at the counter. So when I call, remember the name, BW."

"BW, huh?" she smiled. "I guess I'll wait for that call."

"You do that, sweetheart."

While driving to the funeral she had to make a call. "Amir, this Kenyetta."

"Hey, boss. Everything cool?"

"Yeah but look, tonight I want you to grab a few men and go to Sparkles. When you get there I want you to teach the owner Sam a lesson."

"What kind of lesson? A permanent one?"

"Naw, but one he'll never forget. And make sure he knows the message is from me."

When she arrived at the funeral, she said her good-byes and buried the part of her life Dyson still owned. To her it was time for the next chapter and a part of her hoped her new friend, BW, would be in it.

There's an old saying, be careful what you wish for.

◀┄┄┄▶

PRESENT TIME

"I'm here, Black. Where are you?"

"I'm comin'. Just wait," he says before ending the call.

As I look at the phone my mind wonders. He's different with me and I'm afraid. As I sit in my car, I examine my features in the mirror. I wonder if he's going to reject me and I pray that the beauty he told me I possessed would be enough to keep him.

He drove up next to me and I moved my Gucci purse from the passenger seat of my car.

"Come over here," I smile. "I got the heat on and it's warm inside."

"Get over here and stop fuckin' around," he says.

I pout and say, "I'm comin' now."

I reluctantly get into his black Yukon and wait on his words. "What's up, BW?" I look into his eyes. "Is everything okay?"

"Naw...I gotta be real wit' you 'bout some things." My heart races. "I can't fuck wit' you no more. It's over."

"Huh? Why?" I'm confused at how he's talking to me. It's like he doesn't care. Like we hadn't made love almost everyday since we met. "Did I do somethin' wrong?"

"I'm just not feelin' the situation no more, Kenyetta," his stare is cold. "You got some good pussy and all but you holding back, so I got to let you go."

"Please don't do this. I need you, BW. Whatever you need me to be I will be." I say touching his knee.

"I need a full time woman in my life." Instantly I know what he wants, a child.

"You know what I do, BW. I have the same responsibilities as you do. Having a baby right now doesn't work for me. I have an operation to run."

"And I don't?"

"I'm not sayin' that, baby. I'm just sayin' that now is not the time for me to have a child. Just give us some time to work, please. Don't leave me like this."

"It's over, Kenyetta," he says coldly.

"Please...don't leave me!"

"I said it's over...now get the fuck out of my car."

I try to touch him and he pushes me away again. His rejection stings and I don't know what to do or what to feel. And to think, I'm losing him because I don't want to have a child.

"Is it somebody else?" I say softly, trying not to disobey his wishes. "If there is I'll be better than her. Please."

"If I ask you to leave again, I'ma lay my hands on you," he frowns. "Now get the fuck out of my car."

Gripping my fur coat, I'm disheartened as I push open the door and hop down. The moment my Jimmy Choo's hit the curb, he pulls off and the mud from the melted snow dampens my coat.

"Don't leave...," he continues to drive away and his taillights grow dimmer the farther away he gets.

Immediately I open my phone lid and redial his number. He doesn't answer so I run after his truck.

"BW please!!!!! Don't leave me alone!" I hear my high heels sound off against the wet concrete. "I'm afraid to be alone! Don't leave me! Pleassssssseeeee!"

He doesn't stop and I walk to my car. My pride and heart ache so much that I can't breathe. I need this man like I need the blood in my body to move, and if all he wants is a baby, I'm willing to do what needs to be done to keep him.

CARISSA

"STAY OUT MY LOVE LIFE."

"I'm tired of your shit every time I come to Emerald! You know I have to be here and nothin' has changed just cause we got back together."

"Well what you expect, Carissa?" he says over the phone as I pull up to the community center. "So I'm gonna ask you again. What's up with our relationship, Car?"

"Lavelle, please! If you were so worried about me, you would've stood up for me when Thick made you choose between your family and the business. Or have you forgotten that shit already?" His silence answered my question. "That's exactly what I thought. Just kiss the girls for me, aight? I'll be home when I can."

The line went silent and only the sounds of my boots hitting the pavement were heard. I'm a boss bitch and boss bitches do what they must! He has to recognize that I'm not his little naïve girlfriend anymore.

"Carissa, how many times do I have to apologize for hurting you? I was wrong for lettin' Thick convince me to turn my back on you. And if you don't want me to care about you, we can just end shit right now."

I was about to respond when the call drops.

"Fuck!" I say out loud as I shake my phone and pray for a better signal to call Lavelle back. "I hate Sprint's service!"

"You aight?" Yvette asks jumping up from the table as I enter the meeting. Mercedes was right by her side with the same concerned look on her face.

"Yeah...I'm okay. It's Lavelle. He still trippin' 'bout me runnin' Emerald," I say taking my coat off before joining my friends at the table. "He gotta get over it though."

Yvette sits back down and says, "He just cares about you, Carissa. You might as well get use to it."

"That's some bullshit!" Mercedes yells. She was the only one out of my friends who was still angry about me and Lavelle getting back together. "He shoulda worried when they almost tried to kill us for taking Emerald from them. I'm sick of Cameron and Lavelle runnin' they mouths about what we should do around here."

"Mercedes, stay out my love life," I tell her. "Cause I sure don't get into yours."

"I'm just bein' a friend, Carissa. I'm not the enemy. But if you have a problem wit' me givin' my opinion, then don't worry 'bout it," she says as she pulls her long silky ponytail toward the back. "I'll never do it again."

"Whateva, Mercedes!"

"Whateva then!"

"What the fuck is goin' on?" Yvette asks in an even and steady tone. She looks between us. "Whatever's goin' on ya'll betta end that shit right now. We done been through too much to be arguing over dumb shit. Now both of ya'll have a point but at the end of the day, we still family. I mean...ain't that what you guys just told me out in the yard? And Mercedes you should love her no matter who she wit' cause I would want ya'll to treat me the same no matter who I love."

Yvette's statement was filled with conviction and I felt she wanted to say something else.

Mercedes giggles and says, "Well if you had a man we would treat you the same but you gotta get one first, bitch!"

Yvette laughs and says, "Shut up, winch!"

Looking at me Mercedes continues, "I'm sorry, Carissa."

"I'm sorry too," I tell her managing a light smile.

I knew where her apprehension came from and that's why I bit my tongue. But I love him and he's my man...not to mention we had two little girls together. I still remember the day he told me he couldn't live without me.

◀┈┈┈┈┈┈┈┈┈┈┈┈┈┈┈┈┈┈┈┈┈┈┈┈┈┈┈┈┈┈┈▶

THE NIGHT THICK WAS KILLED

Carissa, Yvette, Kenyetta and Mercedes sat around the table laughing at their ex-boyfriends. The men found it hard to believe that Dreyfus, their former drug supplier, would deal with them considering the lack of respect he had for women.

"Yeah...Dreyfus is somethin' else isn't he?" Yvette said.

"Yes he is...and he doesn't work wit' females," Cameron added.

"Maybe...maybe not," Yvette told him. "All I know is he has a bad ass house. I'm telling you the waterfall was outrageous. What did you think, Mercedes?"

"I don't know, Yvette," she said as she shrugged her shoulders. "I liked his head better. He can suck a mean pussy."

Cameron's face went red out of anger. "Oh so you fuckin' Dreyfus now?"

"Sit down playa," Derrick said. "Slow your roll."

Cameron looked up at him and sat back down.

"And where are my fucking kids while you out tossing pussy at that nigga? Huh? Where my kids?"

Mercedes laughed. "Don't' worry baby...they weren't there."

Cameron wanted to smack the shit out of Mercedes but Lavelle pulled him back down.

"What makes you think we'd just walk away from a million dollar empire?"

"For one we've doubled the salary of our soldiers so they have our backs, and Dreyfus doesn't want to fuck wit' you for your betrayal in Vegas," Yvette told them.

"Ya'll told him about that?" Dyson asked.

"Of course!" Kenyetta laughed.

"And how did ya'll know?" Cameron added.

"Let's just say ya'll should choose the female company ya'll take with you on business trips more wisely in the future." Yvette advised.

Lavelle shook his head in disgust.

"So ya'll have a connection wit' Dreyfus and now we're out huh? Well what about the money we put in this shit? We ain't walkin' away empty handed," Dyson said.

With that, Yvette snapped her fingers and one of the soldiers placed a steel suitcase on the table. She popped open the latches, looked at the money, and turned it around to them.

"It's all there." Yvette assured them sliding the case across the table.

They looked at each other, visibly shook.

"Well what'll happen if we don't buy this shit?" Cameron said.

"Then you'll end up like Thick," Yvette responded.

"And how's that?" Lavelle asked.

Yvette looked around the table. "Dead."

They jumped up from their seats and pulled out weapons as our soldiers placed three barrels to their heads apiece.

"Don't make this nastier then it has to be. You did us wrong and you know it, and now it's time to step down," Yvette said. "Either way somebody loses but don't forget about the kids involved. If you don't step down, somebody will get killed because we won't stop fighting until the last breath leaves our bodies. And that could mean Lil' C without a mother or father. Or what about Lavelle's kids? Everybody loses if these guns pop in here tonight."

"Ya'll have other shops. Ya'll don't need EC," Carissa said.

The look on their faces was that of defeat, remorse and guilt. They knew they had done the women wrong and they deserved Emerald City. No fuck that, they earned it! They also knew if they didn't step down, they were fully prepared for war.

"So what's up? Do you step down or not?" Yvette said.

They looked at each other and grabbed the money off the table without saying a word.

"That was a good decision," Yvette said. "Now can you do us one more solid?"

"And what the fuck is that, Yvette?" Cameron responded still not believing everything that took place. "Take your dead friend with you? He's up in my apartment."

When the men left, the women spent twenty more minutes inside before exiting the building arm and arm.

"We did it girls," Yvette said as the cold air hit them outside. "We fought and we won!"

"Yvette you so fucking smart! You knew this shit would work," Carissa said. "But how were you sure?"

"I'm wasn't. It was a big chance but I was willing to take it," she said.

"Are you sure your face is okay?" Kenyetta asked. "That cut looks pretty deep."

"It ain't deeper than the hurt I felt by Thick's betrayal."

"And how you doing with that situation? Mentally I mean. We know how much you loved him despite of himself." Mercedes asked.

"It hurts. Thick was the first and only man I'd ever been with. I'm fucked up but what can I do? Let him disrespect me and then my friends? Naw," she said shaking her head. "I couldn't see that. I had to push off and what's done is done."

There was silence between them as they moved to the blue Suburban waiting to take them home. Four armed men guarded the truck.

"But did you guys see the looks on their faces?" Mercedes laughed.

"Yeah…they were crushed," Kenyetta responded.

"They should've thought about that before they did us dirty," Mercedes added. "And what about Cameron yelling, 'What about my kids! Who had my kids?' He sounded so stupid!" They all laughed.

"Oh shit!" Carissa said from nowhere. "I left my keys in the community center."

"We'll all go back," Yvette said as they stopped before reaching the truck. "We have to stick together."

"No we don't," she giggled. "We won! It's over now. Anyway you can see the door from here. So get inside the warm truck, pop the bottle of champagne and pour my glass. We'll celebrate when I come back out."

"You sure you don't want one of the soldiers goin' wit' you?" Mercedes persisted.

"I'm sure," Carissa said tapping her arm jogging inside. "It'll only take me a second.

She ran to the office where she left her keys. Once she had them, she was on her way out when she saw Lavelle standing in the doorway.

"Carissa, I have to talk to you."

He looked like the life had been drained from his body and Carissa was angry that she was there alone.

"If you hurt me they'll see you, Lavelle. You won't make it outta here alive!"

"I don't want to hurt you, baby."

"Well what do you want, Lavelle?"

"You. I want you, baby. I'm sorry for all the shit I put you through and if you leave me, I don't know what I will do. I don't think I want to live without you," he said grabbing her hands. "Do you want me to die? Is that what you want?"

Carissa's heart pounded and her stomach churned. She saw the hurt in his eyes as they sat at the table. Although everyone else looked at Yvette during the meeting, Lavelle and Carissa maintained their stare upon each other. She felt his pain and he felt hers. They both wondered how they'd gotten themselves into a situation where their relationship was on the line.

"I'm sorry, I can't, Lavelle," she snatched her hands away from him. "It's over."

She was preparing to leave him when she heard a small thud. Turning around she saw Lavelle on his knees with a gun to his head. *Pop!* Lavelle pulled the trigger and Carissa ran up to him.

"What are you doin'?!" she screamed, as she tried to take the weapon from him.

"I told you if you leave me, none of this shit matters," he was preparing to pull the trigger again until she wrapped her arms around him.

"Please, Lavelle. I do love you but you hurt me so much. I don't want you to do this. Please."

"You don't give a fuck about me so why should I?"

CLICK.

"LAVELLE! Don't do this! I wanted nothing more than to be with you. Why did you have to do this to me and our family?" she said as his head rested firmly on her stomach. He wrapped his arms around her tiny waist, gun still in his hand.

"I was a fool," he wept. "A fuckin' fool and I'm sorry, baby girl. Let me do all the things I said I'd do for you and more. I can be the man you need me to be I promise!"

Carissa listened but wondered about his recent suicide attempt. She doubted if it was real and that any bullets had been placed inside the gun.

"Okay," she said softly. "I'll give you another chance."

"For real?" he said standing up with his hands resting strongly on her shoulders.

"Yes...okay. But you have to be slow with me, Lavelle. I'm not the woman I use to be. This game has changed me. You have changed me," she said taking the gun from his hand removing the clip next.

She stumbled.

It was loaded.

"Lavelle, there's bullets in this gun."

"You thought I was playin'? I don't want to live without you!"

"Lavelle," she cried wrapping her arms around him. "What about our daughters? You were gonna kill yourself and leave our girls?"

"I need all of you. But if I can't have you too, I don't want to live."

They spent a few more moments together and she warned him to wait before leaving the building. If the soldiers saw him coming out they wouldn't hesitate to shoot him.

"I'll stay behind," he said kissing her again. "I snuck back through the side door after getting rid of Thick's body. I just had to see you before I left. Can we talk to-night?"

"Yes. But don't leave right now."

"You've made me a happy man."

"I hope I'm not making a mistake."

"You're not, Carissa. You're not."

When Carissa turned down the hallway to leave him, she ran into Yvette who heard everything.

"So how long have you been waiting?"

"Long enough. When you didn't come back out, I came looking for you."

"Yvette, I'm so sorry," she said softly.

"Don't be. I can tell you still love him. But if he hurts you, I need you to know that I won't hesitate on killing him. Can you handle that?"

"I would have to."

"Cool, 'cause that's on my life. So are you sure?"

"Yes."

"Well it's settled," she said hugging her. "Congratulations."

Yvette kept her secret until Carissa finally decided to reveal it to the rest of her friends who knew all along. It was the last time Carissa said she'd ever lie to her friends.

◀┈┈┈┈┈┈┈┈┈┈┈┈┈┈┈┈┈┈┈┈┈┈┈┈┈┈┈┈┈┈▶

PRESENT

"Anybody seen Kenyetta? She's never late for a meeting?" Yvette says jumping back on topic. "We have a lot to discuss tonight."

Right before we answered, she runs through the door obviously disoriented.

"I'm sorry I'm late," she says sitting down. "It won't happen again." She looks at the confused expressions on our faces. "Please don't ask me what's wrong with me," her head drops and she wipes her face with her hands. "I'm not in the mood right now."

Yvette shrugs her shoulders and says, "Alright let's get started. Where are we with supply Mercedes?"

"I did a check before I got here and the soldiers are stocked and supplied. The stash houses look good for at least another week. Then we have to connect with Dreyfus again."

"Cool...any security issues I should know about?" Yvette questions Kenyetta.

Visibly upset she takes a deep breath and says, "The guards at the gate said that a cop came through here the other night chasin' Aleed. But they shut down the entire operation so the cop didn't find him or anything else."

"A cop came on Emerald's grounds?" I ask.

"Yeah. I said the same thing. But you know the Emerald City crew ran his ass outta here. They think he was a rookie because the vets know the rules. Don't bother us and we won't bother you."

"Wow," Mercedes says shaking her head. "I'm glad he had enough sense to roll out. The squad won't hesitate to kill a cop."

"We don't ever want shit to get that far," Yvette reminds us. "That's unnecessary drama."

"I agree. The vet cops give us our space but if one of their own gets killed, all bets are off." Kenyetta says. "We won't be able to make no money 'round here."

"Exactly," I respond.

"But other then that incident, the fort has been tight," Kenyetta concludes.

"Good, did everybody get paid yesterday?" Yvette ask me.

"Yep...Derrick made sure all the soldiers got hit off. So stop worryin'."

"Don't be too cocky, Carissa. Somethin' could happen at any moment. Just cause things look peaceful don't mean there ain't haters amongst us. I got word back the other day that a few heavy hitters in northwest are out for us." Yvette says.

"You already know that. This is *the* most profitable operation in DC. Wit' the relationships we built and the cops we have on payroll, we virtually unstoppable." Kenyetta says.

"Exactly and that's why we're a target," Yvette responds.

"Be for real, Yvette. Somebody might try us on the outside, but ain't nobody crazy enough to come in Emerald," Mercedes adds.

"Is your ponytail too tight?" Yvette asks. "We should never be caught slippin'. Ever! It's better to be safe than sorry."

I agreed with what Yvette was saying but also understood Mercedes's point. We did everything possible to ensure our operation ran smoothly. From hiring extra lookouts to having our soldiers sent to the gun range twice a month for training. We had more soldiers on payroll than any other project except Tyland. Our fort was tight.

The moment the thought enters my mind, we hear gunfire outside and jump to our feet.

"Fuck was that!" I ask with my hand resting firmly on my 9.

"Wait a minute. Let me call Derrick," Yvette says as we put our coats on.

Derrick was in charge of security and was good at it because his men respected how he worked side by side with them.

"Derrick, what's goin' on?" Yvette asks on her speaker Boost phone.

"We about to see now. Is everybody okay?"

"Yeah, we fine."

"*Everybody*?" he repeats.

"Mercedes is here and she's fine, Derrick. Just let us know what's up."

"Okay," he exhales. "I'ma find out what's goin' on and I'll get back wit' you. Yvette, let me handle this okay?"

"I'm gonna let you handle it, but you know I have to be involved."

"I know, just give me a head start. That's what you hired me for."

"Like I said...I still have to be involved."

"Aight...I'll hit you when I know something," he says hanging up.

"What you think is up?" Kenyetta asks Yvette.

"I don't know, but I think we gonna find out."

It had been years since shots rang in Emerald City that was unrelated to our handing down the law. As I follow my friends to the door, all of us draped in fur coats, something in my spirit told me things were about to change for the worse. And to think, Yvette just said not to be caught slippin'. I guess that's why she's the boss.

EMERALD CITY
LANI & SACHI
"THAT'S FOR FUCKIN' WIT' MY MAN, BITCH!"

"I knew you wouldn't be able to find his pass code!" Sachi says as she sat in the chair next to her twin sister Lani at the computer station.

Two huge canopy beds sat in the middle of the room which was dressed completely in pink. The girls had everything they desired including a 62 inch plasma TV and 22 inch Apple Mac book. Their father Craig sold drugs and lavished his girls with everything they wanted. Developed way beyond their years, twins Sachi and Lani were head turners. With small waists, large round butts and tiny breasts, they were the envy at school. To add to their mystic, the twins both had long golden naturally curly hair.

Sachi and Lani lived in Emerald city with their mother Margaret and father Craig. Although Craig was of the street and always on them, Margaret was also always gone. She was having an affair with her mother's new husband and no one knew. And since they were never home, the girls were always out of control.

"Shut the fuck up, Sachi! Here it goes right here," she says as she hit the enter button and gained access to her boyfriend Lil' C's Myspace account. "I betta not find out he's fuckin' around either."

"And if he is what you gonna do?" Sachi teases. "Take him back as usual?"

"Not this time. Cameron be checkin' for me way more than I be checkin' for him." She continues writing down his pass code on the paper next to their computer.

When Lani reads his messages, she's devastated when she sees one from her best friend Jona. The message reads,

'Lil' C, i hope u liked how i sucked u off at my house yesterday. your cum tastes like my favorite candy. if you want me to do it again, just stop by before you go 2 Lani's. call me first so i can make sure my mother not home. i hope you can cum again. you gonna be mine, 2. i don't care what you say.'

"Oh shit! I should fuck that bitch up!" Sachi says covering her mouth. She paces the room in a burgundy Juicy Couture set. "She a snake!"

Lani rises like a zombie and exits her apartment in Unit D. Marching toward Jona's apartment which is a few doors down, she can't wait to give her a piece of her mind. The pink Baby Phat velour sweat suit she's wearing seems like a blur in a hallway full of people. Her sister is right by her side.

"Don't do nothin' first, Lani! Let me smack her ass!"

Lani bangs on Jona's door forcefully and steps back. She cracks her knuckles and Sachi jumps up and down anxiously. Sachi loves trouble.

"What the fuck...," Jona says flinging the door open.

When the door opens, Lani steps up and shoves the pen she used to write Lil' C's pass code down in her stomach.

"Owwwww!" Jona screams gripping her belly.

Once she falls, Sachi kicks her multiple times in the stomach and face with her black Ugg's.

"That's for fuckin' wit' my man, bitch!" Lani says.

"Dusty, bitch! You betta be glad we ain't kill you!" Sachi adds.

Lil' C and his friend Nicholas, who looks like a young Snoop Dog, steps off the elevator when he sees Lani and Sachi leaving Jona's apartment. He takes a double take when he sees Jona crying on the filthy floor in front of her door. Lil' C who looks like a young Al B. Sure stands in shock and the neighbors crowd in the hallway.

"Aye, what the fuck happened?" Lil' C asks, his curly hair peaking under his fitted New York Yankees cap.

Lil' C is dressed warmly in an extra large blue North Face coat. Nicholas had on a red Eddie Bauer one.

"Damn! Shawty fucked up!" Nicholas adds taking his black knit hat off revealing his soft bushy hair.

"Lil' C, don't start wit' me cause this all your fault. So you betta get in here before I go off on you too," Lani promises in front of her door.

Lil' C and Nicholas take one last look at Jona and follow the girls inside.

"Why are you trippin'?" Lil' C takes off his cap. "You lucky I didn't go off on you in the hallway. But I ain't want my moms gettin' in the business." He wasn't supposed to be in Emerald to begin with.

"So you fuckin' my best friend now?" Lani screams ignoring him. "I told you if I caught you cheating I would go off. So this if your fault!"

Although he liked her for her spiciness, right now she was irritating him.

"First off calm down," Lil' C says calmly. He always maintained his coolness.

"Let me know what you wanna do," Nicholas says with his coat still on. "If you ain't up for this we can roll right now."

"You ain't goin' no where," Sachi says to Nicholas jumping on his lap. Whenever he came over they kept each other company.

"C, why are you fuckin' my best friend? I bet everybody in school knows it!"

"I don't know what you talkin' about."

"So you don't know what *fuckin'* means now?"

"She saw the Myspace account, Cameron. So you might as well stop lying," Sachi says as she and Nicholas turn on 106 & Park.

"Mind your business 'cause you 'bout to make shit worse for your sister," he turns and looks at Lani and says, "I ain't fuckin' wit that girl. So if that's why you did whatever you did to her, I sure hope you can handle the beef when her cousins find out."

"I ain't scared of no Tyland Tower hood rats!"

"I hope so cause you know how they roll."

"What about how you roll?" Lani grabs Lil' C's hand and leads him to her bedroom pointing at the computer screen

"Busted!" she says with her hand on her hips. "'Explain to me why she messagin' you?" she asks pointing her red manicured nail at him.

Lil' C is mad at himself for not deleting his messages. "If I ask you again to lower your voice, I'm outta here," He was trying to figure out how she got his pass code not realizing his birthday would be the first thing she'd try. "And I ain't fuck her. She sucked my dick. There's a difference."

"Boy, are your crazy!" Lani screams.

"You know what," he says leaving her room. "I'm gone." She runs behind him.

"Be a man, Cameron! Don't be a pussy! If you got caught say you got caught!"

"Nick, you ready? Lani's ass is trippin' and I ain't got time for this shit."

Nicholas pushes Sachi off of his lap and stands up, "Let's roll." He places his hat on his head.

"Cameron, why are you leavin'?!" Lani cries as they walk toward the door.

He attempts to pull open the door that wouldn't open and she grabs his arm.

"Get off of me, Lani." He says looking into her eyes. "Don't make me hurt you."

"Just tell me the truth," she sobs. "All I want you to do is tell the truth."

Lani's pain went deeper than what Lil' C realized. With her father being in the street, and her mother never being home, she leaned on him for emotional support. He was the only person other than her sister who she could rely on. In her eyes, he took care of her and she didn't want to lose his love.

"I told you the truth."

"Cameron," she weeps as tears run down her face and snot oozes from her nose. "I don't want to break up."

"It's over," he told her. Lani drops to the floor and goes berserk.

"Unlock this door, Sachi." He says ignoring her antics.

"Fuck you, Cameron," Sachi responds as she bends down and rubs her sister's back. "Why you doin' this to my sister?"

Nicholas's phone rings and he steps to the side to take the call.

"Open this door, shawty." Cameron asks sternly. "I told ya'll to stop lockin' us in here anyway. Who the fuck locks a door with a key from the inside?"

"Not until you apologize, Cameron!"

"That was Ryan," Nicholas interrupts. "they say they got the stuff."

"Already?" Lil' C rises his eyebrows. He sold weed at school behind his parent's backs.

"I know right? He wasn't jokin' when he said he could come through."

"That's what's up," he smiles. "Uh, Sachi, I'ma need you to let us out now. We got shit to do."

"All you care about is sellin' drugs! Why you out there you need to know she's pregnant. Now what's up?" The room was silent for a moment.

"Pregnant?!" he says looking down at Lani.

"Yes! And you the father!" Sachi adds.

"Why you say somethin', Sachi?!" Lani asks wiping her tears.

"Cause he need to know!"

"Is it true? You havin' my kid?"

"Why? It ain't like you care! All you wanna do is fuck my best friends!"

He was about to speak when gunfire rang outside. The first person he thought about was his mother.

"Damn! What was that?" Nicholas asks looking toward the window.

"I gotta call my peoples," Lil' C says removing his cell phone from his pocket.

"Who?"

"My moms." He was preparing to speed dial her number.

"Hold up! You not supposed to be in Emerald," he stops him. "If you call her she's gonna know your here."

Reluctantly he places the phone back in his pocket. First he finds out his girl is pregnant and now shots ring out in his mother's kingdom. The day wasn't going as planned but what he didn't realize was, it was about to get worse.

EMERALD CITY

"IF SOMETHIN' HAPPENS, I'M HOLDIN' YOU BOTH RESPONSIBLE."

Derrick rushes out of the Unit C apartment he had in Emerald City with his heavy blue North Face coat filled with a desert eagle and Glock 9mm loaded and ready for action. When he enters the hallway, people are standing around looking nervously about the gunshots.

"What's goin' on, Derrick?" asks an elderly lady. Her red cat walks from out of her apartment and into the hallway. Although she despises the idea of drugs being sold in Emerald, she took comfort in how safe things became since the girls had taken over. "I heard shots and I'm worried. Are the girls okay?"

"Everything's okay, Miss Key," he says picking up her cat and handing it to her. "Try not to worry."

The woman grabs her furry cat and looks to him for more information. But Derrick moves through the hallway and toward the elevator feeling more like a policeman than an dealer.

"Are you sure, son?" Miss Key calls to him.

"Positive," he says confidently.

"Don't lie to her!" Yells the crazy old man down the hall. He always ranted and raved about the future and the danger that would come to Emerald. "This is the start of hell here on earth! And it's all you drug banger's faults!"

"Get ya, old ass down the hall and stop trippin!" Derrick says looking at the man who was dressed in a brown pair of khaki pants with a white wife beater. His nipples peaking out on the sides. "Don't nobody wanna hear that shit!"

"It's true! Everyone's goin' to hell!" Derrick ignores him and waits impatiently for the elevator.

"Fuck!" he says pushing the button to the elevator again. It wasn't coming fast enough for him.

"Derrick, is everybody okay?" asks Bucky, a beautiful dark skin girl who'd been trying to get with him for the longest. Although it was cold outside, she chose to walk into the hallway wearing a tight pair of blue jean shorts with a ripped up t-shirt. Every curve on her body was defined and exposed. "Cause I heard gunshots and I'm scared."

"Everything's cool. And you know not scared so stop faking," he tells her trying not to look at her thick thighs and fat ass.

"I don't know why you think I'm so strong," she says touching his arm. "If I had you though, I wouldn't have to worry."

"Well you don't got me," he says shaking his head. Bucky stares him down licking her lips.

"Not now but I will," she responds wiggling toward her apartment.

Derrick was relieved when the elevator finally opens. When he gets downstairs, his men are waiting.

"What happened?" he asks Bruce, Paul, Harold and Ed as they follow him to the building's door.

"We were out here on post, when somebody said some niggas was tryin' to come through the gate. Next thing I know, the Unit B crew starts bustin' off. I ain't seen nothin' else cause we ran upstairs to get you."

Derrick phone rings and its Mercedes. "What's up?"

"Is everything cool?" She asks.

"Naw...somethin' is up," he tells her. "Maybe you should go home until everything blows over." He knows she won't leave.

"We on our way out," she says hanging up.

"Let's go to the guard's station," he tells his men.

When they get there, they see blood pouring from the large window of the guard's station. There was broken glass and meaty matter everywhere. They all aim and walk closer. They see Jake murdered and the gate left unsecure. All that remained was a uniformed body with no head. He wonders how many outsiders were in the city.

"Bruce...I want you and Paul to stay right here and watch the gate. Don't let nobody come through you don't know. I'ma have somebody, get Jake out of here."

"Got it!" Bruce says stealing a few looks at the bloody carnage.

"Harold and Ed, ya'll come with me."

"Let me and Ed watch the gate," Harold asks.

"Yeah...we got it!" Ed chimes in.

"What you sayin', I won't watch the city right?" Bruce responds.

"Naw, but we know you won't watch the city like we will."

"Aight, ya'll got it, but if somethin' happens, I'm holdin' you both personally responsible." They nod in agreement. "Come on," he says to Bruce and Paul.

Looking up to the rooftop, Derrick notices something is out of order. Where were the sharp shooters? Where were the soldiers on the field? Safety had been breeched and Emerald city was in major jeopardy. Times were changing...for the worse.

YVETTE

"WE SHOULD'VE NEVER ABANDONED OUR POSTS."

"How this happen?" Yvette asks Derrick as they stand on the steps of Unit C.

The soldiers were back in position on the field and the shooters were back on the roof. By the looks of things, it appeared that Emerald City was in order. But the trained eye could tell that things were far from normal.

"I talked to Aleed and a few others. They said a van packed with a rack of niggas pulled up trying to get in but Jake wouldn't open the gate. They said one of the niggas got out, ran up to him and fired. Jake couldn't even call and warn us. After that, one of the dudes in the van opened the guard's station and then the gate. They all ran in after that."

"Where were the shooters on the roof?" Mercedes asks.

"They said everyone on our crew ran after the men, including the rooftop soldiers. Aleed told me about twenty dudes got in. When they looked for the men, they were gone. It's like they disappeared into the walls of the city."

"The soldiers in the field left post too?" I ask.

"Everybody went after these cats, Yvette. It's fucked up but it's true," he says dropping his head.

"This was a fuckin' set up!" I say walking away from them momentarily. "They knew if they ran through, we'd leave the gate empty and abandon our posts. We should've never abandoned our posts, Derrick!"

"I know," he says. "But what else could they do? Just let 'em run in without *trying* to do something?"

"He's right, Yvette," Mercedes says.

"I know it's fucked up but we never had a situation like this happen and the men weren't prepared. I take responsibility for that. But trust...it'll never happen again," Derrick responds.

I knew what he was saying was true, but it didn't eliminate our problem.

"You think they still here?" Carissa asks.

"I know they are," I say looking around. I feel violated.

"What now?" Mercedes asks.

"Let's question the neighbors. They might not tell the cops if they seen somethin', but they'll tell us. We just have to make sure we protect them."

I was still talking to my crew when Chris, my lesbian lover, walks outside of the building. She looks worried and my heart drops when I see her coming straight for me.

"Who the fuck is this dyke?" Mercedes asks. "I see her all the time but she ain't always live here."

"Yeah...I was thinkin' the same thing?" Carissa adds. "Fuckin' carpet munchin' ass bitch probably got somethin' to do wit' this shit."

Although concrete can't melt, I feel as if I'm sinking into the steps. Not only were my friends talking about her like she was less than human, something about their words made me feel dirty.

"Yvette, you okay?" Chris asks moving toward me. "What's goin' on?"

"Bitch, you betta back the fuck up!" Kenyetta says, blocking her from approaching me and extending her hands out in front of her. "I don't know who you are, but you in the wrong place at the wrong time."

"Look, I'm not trynna hurt her. I'm just trynna make sure she's aight."

I can't move or talk. I always wondered if she ever approached me while with my friends, how I'd handle it. I guess I know how.

"Yvette, you not gonna say nothin'?" she says. "You not gonna tell 'em?"

Derrick eyes widen as he examines the situation with his hand on his heat.

"Excuse me, right now is not the time," he interrupts. "So why don't you just go upstairs before things get out of hand."

Chris looks at him hard at first and suddenly her expressions softens.

"Oh…aight…as long as everything cool," she says looking at me again. "I wasn't trynna cause no trouble. Lada, Yvette."

She walks away.

"Yvette, you know her?" Mercedes questions as Chris enters the building.

"Yeah, she acted like she knew you," Kenyetta adds.

"No. I don't know her," I lie denying the love of my life.

Only when she walks away do I breathe again. I can't help but wonder if I lost the best thing that ever happened to me, for good.

KENYETTA

"WHAT I WAS DOING WAS FUCKED UP!"

"Where you go, Kenyetta?" Mercedes asks as I pull up to the damaged guard's station, trying to reenter Emerald. "We were lookin' for you everywhere." Ed and Harold stand guard while she talks to me.

"I know," I say hoping my secret doesn't reveal himself in the back seat of my car concealed behind tinted windows. "I just needed to get away for a minute."

"Well you can't be doin' shit like that right now," she says. "We're at war, Kenyetta. Yvette is out lookin' for you right now."

"Tell her I'm cool. But look, let me go inside and I'll be back out in a little."

"You sure you cool?" Harold and Ed look at me, smirk and laugh. I wonder what that means.

"Yeah. I'm fine. Really."

I pull off before she can object causing the sound of my wheels rolling on the gravel and dirt to penetrate my betrayal. What I was doing was fucked up! I'm bringing a member of the Tyland Tower crew onto Emerald City grounds. What surprised me the most was that he agreed to lay hidden under a thick blanket as I drove through our gates and behind Unit B.

When we park, I get out and he follows minutes later as we enter my apartment. I made him wear a hoodie to conceal his face. Once inside, I say, "Make yourself comfortable, I'ma get cleaned up."

"You know this some gangsta shit right?" he says taking off his hood.

I smile. "Give me a minute, baby." I gently kiss his mouth and leave.

When I come out of the bathroom ten minutes later, he's stretched out in my bed.

"You gonna stare or are you gonna come over here and lay down next to me?" he says stroking his hard dick. He got comfortable real quick.

"I'm comin', baby," I say seductively.

For some reason, as I walk slowly toward him, I grow nervous. My mind says this is not something I should do, but my heart and body call for him. When I make it to the bed, I ease on top of him. He grabs my waist and pulls me onto him until my pussy surrounds his dick like a glove. My head falls back as he pushes into me.

"Damn, Kenyetta," he moans. "Why this pussy wet already?"

I don't tell him that I played with my pussy before coming out to get in the mood. I didn't want to risk having painful sex because of not being able to get into the act. After all, I'm betraying my best friends.

"You gonna carry my seed, Kenyetta?" He says looking at me.

"Yes," I say as I push down so hard, not even air could pass between where our bodies connect. "I'ma carry your baby."

We went at it for about an hour and my pussy was raw. BW never did cum right away. I decide to step up my dirty talk to bring him closer to ecstasy.

"Fuck this pussy, baby!"

"You want me to fuck it?"

"Yeah...I want you to fuck the shit out of this wet pussy!"

"You sexy ass, bitch! I'ma knock the walls out of this shit!"

"Fuck me, daddy! Fuck your little girl!"

That really does it for him because he shakes and I know he's about to cum. As he's preparing to ejaculate inside of me, I get scared. I can't do this! I can't have his baby. My friends don't even know about him yet and he hasn't committed himself to me.

"Do you belong to me?"

"W...what?" he replies on the verge busting his creamy load inside my body.

"I said, are you mine?"

When he doesn't respond I lift off of him and sit by his side. Not trying to lose the sensation, he jerks himself until his sperm rests on his stomach.

With his breaths still heavy he says, "So you playin' games now?"

"No!" I say shaking my head. "Look at what I risked by bringing you here."

"Why did you bring me here if you weren't gonna do what you said?" he frowns.

"Cause you said this was the only way you'd be back with me. I want to be with you, Black." I touch his leg. "I just need to be sure you're mine before I have this baby."

"The baby gonna be takin' care of, Kenyetta." He sits up in the bed and rests the back of his head against the wall.

"I'm not concerned about that. We both have money, but I want to be sure you'll be in the baby's life."

"If I have a kid wit' you, trust me, I'm gonna be in the kid's life. Trust me."

"What about me? Would you always be in my life?"

"I take care of all my kid's mothers. Trust me."

Did he just say, *'all my kid's mothers'*? Far as I know, he doesn't have any kids.

"What do you mean all of your kid's mothers?"

"Look what you wanna do? I'm sick of playin' games."

"You never told me you had kids."

"I'm outta here," he says standing up to get dressed. "I'm riskin' my life and now you gonna renege on a promise?"

"I don't mean to renege on anything but you never told me you had a family."

"Kenyetta, don't call me until you serious." He storms out of my apartment.

My head drops in frustration and I wonder about everything he's ever said to me. I am so confused that I forget he couldn't be seen leaving my apartment or the building. As a member of Tyland Towers, he would be killed *instantly* if spotted, especially with everything that's happening now. I hop off the bed and rush toward the living room. And when I open the apartment, I see Yvette standing in my doorway.

"You aight?" she asks. Sweat pours down my face and I push past her to look out the door.

"Kenyetta, are you aight?" she repeats following my stare.

"Oh...yeah...uh...I'm fine," I say glancing down the hallway. I see no signs of him and walk back inside "What's up?"

"Did Mercedes tell you I been lookin' for you?" she asks standing in the doorway.

"Yes."

"Well?"

"Well what?"

"We waitin' on you at Unit C, Kenyetta. Why you not there?"

"I'm sorry, Yvette. I got in here and got turned around. But I'm comin' now."

"Are you sure?" She looks at my negligee. "It looks like you 'bout to go to sleep."

"Oh...no...I was just taking a quick nap. I'm fine now."

"A nap? Now?"

"Yes. But just give me a few minutes. I'll be down."

"We need you to be focused, Kenyetta. A lot of shit happenin'. And something tells me people we think we can trust are hidin' them niggas on our grounds. Are you wit' us or not?"

"Don't ask what you already know."

"Well prove it."

I exhale and say, "I'll meet you at Unit C, Yvette. Just give me a few moments."

"Aight," she says. "Call me if you need me."

When she leaves I close the door and lean up against it. Sliding to the floor, I try to regain my composure. Ever since Dyson left me, I've been afraid to be alone. Afraid to live my life. Dyson took care of me and protected me even with all of our problems. Still, I know BW is not the man for me. He's a liar. Being by myself so long has given me some time to see clearer. I'll say this, I will never love another again. *Ever*. Love doesn't work for me, and its best not to care.

BLACK WATER

"THEY HAVE LOYALTY TO NO ONE."

Black hurriedly walks away from Kenyetta's apartment before she can spot him. He had planned to enter Emerald anyway with his men in the van. He needed to see the layout of the city for *himself* to be able to plan his attack. So when she said she wanted to see him, he pressed the issue about it being tonight knowing she was there. He couldn't get inside any safer than having an Emerald City boss herself drive him in.

Black Water arrives at Harold's door and knocks twice, the hood of his jacket is still on. One of his Tyland Tower crew members opens the door and he walks inside. All of his men are present. Although the twenty men were only inside for a couple of hours, the smell from the small apartment sickens his stomach.

"Fuck took you so long to answer the door?" he asks Jam J, after slapping him upside the head.

"Owwww!" he rubs his head. "I opened it the moment you knocked."

"Next time move quicker. Somebody coulda spotted me."

"Everybody get the fuck off the couch," Once the space is clear, he sits down.

"So tell me what's up?" he says looking at everyone.

Most of his men were young and expendable. He didn't care if he lost not one of their lives. His best men were still in Tyland safe and sound.

"Forty Deuce, and Money Marter got shot. Them Emerald City boys got 'em when we were trying to get in," Cristal, the youngest member said.

"Where are they now?"

"Reds was fuckin' wit' some chick in this building and she drove them to the hospital."

"They have any problem gettin' out the gate?"

"Naw...Harold on duty."

"Cool, what ya'll know 'bout this bitch?"

"Who? Red's girl?" Jam J asks.

"Naw your mother's bitch!" Black Water yells. The men chuckle.

"Oh...far as I know she cool. I think her name is Goldie or somethin'."

"Okay, I'ma have Harold kill her when she get's back. No witnesses. And after Emerald's mine, I'ma kill Harold and Ed's cause they have loyalty to no one."

Jam J nods his head in agreement. "So what's the plan?" he asks.

"I'ma need three of you tonight. And the rest of you are gonna lay low for a couple of days. Harold and Ed gonna make sure you greedy mothafuckas get whatever you need to eat. And when it's time, we move to plan B."

"Okay," Jam J says as the other men nod.

"Hey, boss...how you get in?" Cristal asks.

"I convinced one of the bitches of Emerald City Squad to let me fuck her in her crib. She drove me right through the gate." Black Water chuckles.

"Damn! Which one was it?" Jam J questions. "Cause I'd fuck any one of 'em."

"Don't worry 'bout all that. Just don't move an inch unless you hear *my* word."

"We got it. How you gonna get out?" Jam J responds.

"Ed gonna meet me 'round back and ride me out."

He told them the plan for later that night. His plan would be the perfect diversion for him to leave Emerald's gates. When he was done giving orders, he thought about the original Emerald City squad. *How in the fuck did the Emerald City Squad give up their project to these bitches? Taking Emerald was gonna be like taking candy from a baby.* He thought.

Picking up his phone he decides to call, Cameron. "I'm inside Emerald."

"That was quick."

"Once I make a decision to do something, I move. And you were right about them dudes Harold and Ed. They looked out in a major way."

"Good. So what's your next move?"

"I gotta work some things out and then I'll get back at you."

"How long will that be?"

"Soon. Why? You havin' a change of heart or somethin'?"

"No! I want this shit to go down just like you do."

"So what's the problem?"

"I just want you to call me before you kill the girls."

"Why?"

"Just call me."

"You'll know before I do anything," Black Water tells him with a smirk on his face.

He ends the call.

"Niggas need to know who they can trust before doin' business." He says to himself. "A lesson this weak ass nigga is about to learn."

CARISSA

"YOU GOTTA LOT OF GROWIN' UP TO DO, CHIC. WE NOT KIDS NO MORE."

The cold air rips through my body as I stand on the steps of Unit C. It has been a long time since we had to man our post ourselves. Even when we came back once a month, we always had our men watching over things for us. But with the recent turn of events we didn't trust this job to anyone else.

As I look around the city, I already miss the five bedroom home I share with Lavelle in Virginia. I'd become accustomed to luxurious living and Emerald was far from my new reality.

"Kenyetta, that shit can't work," I tell her looking at the tiny tube filled with yellow liquid.

"I'm telling you it does. Just one drop will put a nigga straight out of his misery."

"When would you use some shit like that and how did you get it?" I ask.

"You know I go to this acupuncturist," she explains. "She makes it herself. She says most of her clients use it to get some sleep and two drops will put you out for two hours. But I'ma take eight drops. I need to get some rest."

"I don't know why," I laugh. "We won't be getting a lot of rest for the next couple of weeks."

"I know...I'm talkin' about when I go home."

"What's on your mind that you want to be sleep for a whole day?"

"You can't even imagine," she says.

"So what up wit' you and Lavelle?" Mercedes asks me.

"Do you really wanna know?" I sit on a metal chair and tuck my hands further in my coat pockets.

"I wouldn't ask you if I ain't wanna know," she smiles standing beside me.

"If you must know, Lavelle's still upset about me being here. And somebody hot boxed and told him 'bout the shootin' earlier."

"I wonder who said somethin'," Kenyetta responds.

"Who knows," I shrug. "Whether ya'll wanna believe it or not, some of our men still respect Lavelle and Cameron and keep in contact with them."

"I know. That's what bothers me," Kenyetta says.

"It shouldn't. It'd be the same way if you took over a company and kept the existing employees. Some people gonna like old management, and others gonna like the new ones. Some niggas actually think we don't run things as good as the guys did."

"Fuck that! Even when they was runnin' shit we still ran shit! And let's not forget that we pay them better than they ever did. We good to them," Mercedes adds.

"Exactly," Kenyetta says. "Look how long we held shit down wit' out error. It's been years! I bet they ain't talkin' 'bout that shit."

"I wanna know why niggas stay in our business. We ain't fold now and we not gonna fold later," Mercedes says standing up. She looks around at all of the men we had standing in the field and on the roofs. "We too strong for that."

"Mercedes have you forgotten about what happened earlier?" I remind her. "They ran right up in here wit' nothing to stop them."

"Trial and error. We tight now and it's back to business!" Mercedes says.

For some reason, Mercedes and me had been going at it a lot lately and I had a feeling she was jealous that Lavelle was the only one who kept his promise and remained true and loyal. I know she misses Cameron.

"You gotta lot of growin' up to do, chic. We not kids no more. We mothers and we have responsibilities. Stop bein' so immature."

"I'm immature because I believe that Emerald will stay strong no matter what? I'm not ready to tuck tail and run at the first sign of danger."

"And neither am I!" I yell.

"Are you sure? Cause you sound weak right about now."

"Mercedes, all I'm sayin' is that we need to be smart. I would die for Emerald if I had to, and I know you know that. But I don't wanna die over no stupid shit."

"Okay, Carissa. Whatever you say," she says waving me off.

"Where's Yvette?" Kenyetta asks in an attempt to skip the subject.

"She said she had to go inside to get somethin' to eat," I say still looking at Mercedes. She was workin' my nerves tonight. "But that was like an hour ago."

"Yeah it has been a minute. Should we check on her?" Mercedes replies.

"Naw. As long as three of us are here at a time, we good," I tell her.

"I wish somebody told me that when I went inside," Kenyetta pouts. "Ya'll acted like yall was gonna die without me here."

"That was 'Vette," I say.

And all of a sudden, I notice the expression from one of our men on the rooftop. He looks horrified. I see him draw his gun from his waist, and I follow his stare. When I do, I see three men running quickly in our direction.

"Watch out!" I yell as I draw my weapon.

Kenyetta and Mercedes pull out theirs and we all start firing. The men on the roof and the ones in the field fire as well. Why would these suicidal niggas try us? Bullets rang from everywhere and before long two of them fall. We continue to fire when all of a sudden one of my girls yelp in pain.

"Owwwwwww!" she yells.

Terrified, I can't bring myself to look at who it was. Filled with rage, I hop down the stairs two and three at a time. I want his life with disregard for my own.

"Boss, get outta the way!" one of the men yells from the roof.

I don't stop running until I'm directly in front of him. Bullets stop flying behind me too. I know they are trying to avoid hittin' me. I walk up to him with warm tears streaming down my face. He's a kid. About nineteen or twenty years old and he possibly killed my friend. When I look at his expression, he appears demented. He's on something for sure. I raise my arm and my gun.

He laughs and says, "Fuck you, you crazy-," before he finishes I fire and hit him in the center of his face. He falls.

His blood splatters on my face and white Dior coat. At my feet, I watch the blood rush from his body. Not satisfied, I shoot him a few more times until my gun can only produce a *click click* sound. It was my first time killin' someone but I'm sure it wouldn't be my last. When the high I felt from his death passes, I'm left with the horror of finding out which of my friends are injured. Or dead.

Turning around, I slowly take the walk toward the steps of Unit C. And all of a sudden the sensation I felt when I lost Dex and Stacia overcomes me. Was I about to lose another friend? I feel light as I move and it's as if I'm not walking anymore. The moment I take another step, I pass out on the ground.

YVETTE

"I SHOULD'VE NEVER LEFT MY FRIENDS' SIDE."

"What you want me to do, Chris? I can't just up and tell people I'm a lesbian!" I cry as I watch her fold and pack her clothes on the kitchen table. My body feels like it's sinking into the large chocolate leather sofa I'm sitting on.

"Yvette, you ain't gotta do shit," she says grabbing a folded shirt from the pile, placing it neatly in her suitcase. "You made your decision already."

When everything is packed, she walks toward the bathroom. I quickly follow.

"Chris, please...give me some time!" I say grabbing her arm. "I can't just tell my friends about us overnight! I'm not like you! I haven't been gay all my life."

"Fuck off me, Yvette! You had two years to deal with being gay. But I know what it really is," she says moving toward the living room to grab her coat from the closet.

"What is it?"

"You never had any intentions on telling them about us. You just wanted me to lick your pussy and stay under your bed like some fuckin' sex slave! That shit ain't for me! And that ain't for us! Find another sucka ass bitch. I'm outta here!"

She was just about to leave when I hear multiples gun shots outside. It sounds like war was taking place in the yard. Rushing toward my table I grab my Glock and push past Chris. I was so scared I didn't stop to grab my coat. It had to be about thirty degrees outside. My adrenaline was pumping and suddenly the time I wasted on Chris felt stupid.

I decide against the elevator and take my chances running down the stairs. My heart races as I imagine the worse. I should've never left my friends' side during one of the most dangerous times in Emerald. As I open the door to the building, the first person I see is Carissa being helped upstairs by two of our men. Her facial expression scares me and my heart sinks. Holding the pit of my stomach, I see Mercedes lying on the ground with Kenyetta above her crying.

"Mercedes!" I scream rushing to her side. "How the fuck did this happen?!"

The soldier in me wanted answers but my love for Mercedes prevents me from running through the city and shooting anybody with the slightest look of guilt on their face. Stooping down, I hover over top of her. Her eyes open and she looks scared.

"What happened, Kenyetta?" I ask.

"We were on the steps and these niggas started runnin' toward us firin'."

I'm so angry my hand is shaking and I place my gun in the back of my pants to prevent from firing by mistake.

"Mercedes...where are you hit?"

"In my arm. It burns a little but I'm fine."

I open the blue North face coat she's wearing to check the wound. She moans a little in discomfort as blood pours from her body and onto the concrete.

"I can't watch this," Carissa says as she turns around.

Lifting up her t-shirt, I see her torn flesh in her upper arm.

"Oh shit, Yvette! We gotta call the ambulance," Kenyetta says.

"No! It'll be too hot," Mercedes replies. "Plus we have to get rid of the bodies."

"She's right. Let's get her to Old Lady Faye's house downstairs," I tell them as I motion for two of the guys to help pick her up. They run upstairs.

"Kenyetta, call the Vanishers and have them remove the bodies off the field."

The Vanishers were our best kept secret. Whenever we wanted a body gone, they would come in this black beaten up van, and take the body off of Emerald City grounds. I don't know how they disposed of the remains, but the bodies were never found.

"Carissa, tell the lieutenants we have an emergency meeting in two hours at the community center. Shit is about to get serious around here."

"Huh?" she says staring off into space, disoriented.

"Carissa, you hear me?" I reply walking up to her.

She doesn't move. I guess all of the action must've been too much for her. But as far as I was concerned she would have to get use to it because things were about to get real nasty. The fuckin' games are over.

"Carissa, wake the fuck up!" I say smacking her in the face. She rubs her skin and looks into my eyes. "I said tell the lieutenants we have a meeting in two hours. I need you wit' me so man the fuck up!"

"Oh...okay. I'll call everybody now."

"We ready to take her to Faye's." the men say holding Mercedes in their arms.

"Cool, I'll be down to check on you later, Mercedes."

"Okay."

After my orders were given, I turn around to see Chris standing there.

"You okay?" she asks in a concerned tone.

I want to lie and say no thinking she'd stay. I look around to see who's watching but there's so much going on and everyone is so preoccupied with Mercedes that they don't notice Chris was in my face for the second time that day.

"I'm fine," I say softly keeping my voice down. "You sure you wanna do this?"

"I'm sure I gotta do this, Bye, Yvette," she responds walking down the stairs.

"Mercedes!" I hear Derrick screaming as he runs up the stairs and toward us mad as hell.

There's commotion everywhere but for the moment, all I see is Chris walking away. Even Derrick's distraught voice disappears as he rushes past me. I want to beg her not to take another step away but I can't. She's gone and my soul misses her already.

BLACK WATER

"IF WE GONNA MOVE WE GOTTA MOVE NOW."

The room is almost completely dark with the exception of the light illuminating from the clock and bathroom light. The fan above the huge brass bed cooled Black Water's body. Half sleep, he grips his wife's slender leg when she places it over his. After the sex-capade they had the night before, they were beat.

Shade Holman had been married to Jesse Holman, also known as Black Water since she was seventeen. And now that she was 34, she'd bore him twelve children including his sixteen year old son favorite son, Tamir. Her body showed no signs of birth. Her beautiful dark skin and long silky hair transferred to all of her children.

Black was careful about picking the right women to bare his kids. He wanted his offspring as beautiful as their mothers. And had he not bought out Dreyfus for twenty million, to own Tyland, the women he picked would've been unattainable to such an unattractive man. But his power, and swag, made him appealing.

When the phone rings at seven in the morning, it startles Shade a little. "Mmmmm, baby, you expectin' any calls?" she purrs gripping him. Her hair falls down her back and her fingers are covered in diamonds.

"Naw," he says groggily. "Answer it."

"Hey, Shannon…Get the phone," Shade tells her sister who's also in the bed on the other side of Black.

Although Shannon was also Black's wife, their marriage was not legal. Shade managed to convince Shannon to participate in the marriage the moment she was eighteen because Black wanted her the moment he saw her. At first Shannon refused cursing the idea of sleeping with the same man as her sister. But when she was presented with a custom colored pink Rolls Royce on her nineteenth birthday it sealed the deal.

Shannon was two years younger than her older sister Shade. And just like Shade, she possessed the same silky hair which she kept neatly locked. The sisters' body frames were totally different. Shade was tall with large breasts and Shannon was short with a fat ass and beautiful brown eyes. Shannon had given him ten children.

Black didn't lie to his wives and he always made his plan clear. He wanted to wife as many women as possible so that they could birth his children. And for their participation, he lavished them with anything they desired. He wanted an army which he called the Black Water Clan. His quest for power consumed him.

Shannon complies rolling over to answer the phone. "Hello?"

"Is Black there?" Cameron asks.

"Who's calling?"

"Tell him it's Cameron. I need to talk to him right now."

"Baby, it's Cameron,'" she says holding the cordless phone. "He says it's important."

Black sits up in the bed and angrily accepts the phone. Shade and Shannon rub and kisses his chest. The diamonds on their hands stand out against his dark skin.

"This betta be good," Black says as his wives' caresses causes him to grow hard. His chest was his hot spot and they knew it.

"What the fuck is goin' on in Emerald?!"

"I don't know what the fuck you talkin' about but I ain't one of your bitches! Now I think you better calm down a little, partner and explain. 'Cause this sounds like a misunderstandin' and that shouldn't be when we 'bout to make money together."

Cameron takes a deep and says, "Mercedes was shot last night."

"I don't know shit about that. Sounds to me like you callin' the wrong dude."

"Well who was it then?"

"Look...niggas get shot all the time in this game. Just cause they got pussies don't make them immune. But whateva happened to her was not by my hands. Give me some time, I might be able to find out what went down later."

"Yeah well I need to know quick."

"Like I said, I'll check on that and get back wit' you." Black was desperately trying to maintain his composure. For now, he still needed Cameron. "Did you get things together wit' your peoples in Emerald? If we gonna move we gotta move now."

"What peoples?"

"Cam, you aight ? Cause you actin' irrational right now."

"I'm fine, nigga." Cameron barked.

"Good. Now what's up wit' your crew in Emerald? Are they ready?"

Cameron still mad Mercedes got shot says, "Yeah. They waitin' on my word."

"So when you gonna give it? Or are you gonna let bullshit get in the way of business?"

"When you tell me what went down last night, I'll place the call. Not 'til then." Cameron says hanging up the phone.

As Black lay in the bed he was trying to avoid having him killed. He didn't feel like receiving calls over a bitch the nigga said he wanted dead.

"Don't worry 'bout that dumb shit, baby," Shade coos.

"Yeah, big daddy. You still the man and that nigga betta be glad you even let him in your world," Shannon adds feeding his already large ego .

Black knew his wives were right, but he was still heated. Cameron was accusing him of something he didn't do and was threatening his plans.

◄┄┄┄┄┄┄┄┄┄┄┄┄┄┄┄┄┄┄┄┄┄┄┄┄┄┄┄┄┄┄┄┄►

THE NIGHT BEFORE

"Get the tires too!" Cristal said to one of Black's men.

"This shit can't get more fucked up than this," Jam J laughed looking at the ruined black Dodge Magnum. One of the rearview mirrors was hanging off the car, and scratches and dents were everywhere. "Call Ed and tell him we done."

"Bout time!" Cristal said dialing his number. "We almost got caught twice."

It took Ed two minutes to drive his black Honda from the guard's station to the back of Unit B. Ed parked his car, opened his door and walked toward Carson.

"Carson, I think somebody fucked your car up man," Harold told him while smoking a blunt. "You betta check that shit out. It don't look too good."

"What?" he asked leaning on the wall next to the back door. "Ain't nobody crazy enough to fuck wit' my shit 'round here."

"Apparently we got niggas in Emerald who ain't from 'round here."

Carson wiped his hand over his face in frustration and said, "So you serious?"

"Dead serious, homie. I was drivin' to my crib when I saw that shit."

"Fuck!" he said rubbing his hands over the top of his head. "So you just drivin' around the city and saw my shit, huh?" He nods yes. "I thought you and Harold was 'spose to stay on post." Carson didn't trust Ed. "The bosses said everyone works."

"Look man, I was makin' a run to my crib to get some smoke. The bosses wouldn't even miss me unless somebody told 'em. You not gonna tell 'em, are you?"

"I ain't no snitch, nigga."

"Okay then. I'm lookin' out for you, but if you don't want me to, that's cool."

Ed was preparing to leave hoping he'd stop him and he did.

"Hold on!" Carson yelled. "Can you watch my post while I check on my shit?"

"I'll watch it for you, but you gotta hurry up back."

Carson thought about it for a moment and jogged to the location where he left his car. Ed waited for him to be completely out of view before calling Black Water.

"You can come out, Black. The post is clear."

When Black came out, he hurried to Ed's car and dove in the back seat. Without altercation, Ed drove past Harold at the gate. Since Tyland was only a few blocks up, when he dropped Black off no one noticed he'd left. When he came back, he discovered Mercedes had been shot. Turns out he could not have gotten Black out of Emerald at a better time.

◄┄┄┄┄┄┄┄┄┄┄┄┄┄┄┄┄┄┄┄┄┄┄┄┄┄┄┄┄┄►

THE PRESENT

"Don't worry about that shit, baby," Shannon says. "Worry about this pussy and charge the rest to the game." She continues to stroke his thickness.

"Handle it," he tells her.

Without complaining, she throws back the covers so he can see her putting in work. He loved to watch getting his dick sucked. Shannon always could suck his dick better than her sister or any of his wives for that matter. That's why she was favored.

"Shade, tell Energy to make me some breakfast," he says referring to his third wife who was in the other bedroom sleep.

"No problem," she says smacking her sister on the ass, before exiting the bedroom wearing only her royal blue panties.

Energy was Black's third out of ten wives. Although Energy was beautiful, she wasn't as sexy as his nine other wives. Energy was so light skin she could past for white and the five children she bore all looked like her with silky long hair and light green eyes. But because she could cook her ass off, Black allowed her to stay in his apartment with the sisters. His other wives lived in the same building and on the same floor.

Since everyone had their duties, things ran smooth between them. Black didn't allow bickering, fussing and fighting between his wives. Shade, Shannon and Energy tended to his immediate needs while the other seven took care of the children. No children were allowed to stay in the apartment with him, not even their own. Energy never said it out loud, but she was jealous of the attention he gave the sisters. But she knew if she disputed, she might lose her position as the third favorite. Because her sex was average, she rarely had the honor of sleeping with Black. It hurt hearing the lovemaking sessions at night by the three of them while she lie alone, playing with her own pussy until she went to sleep. Secretly she was building her children up to become the strongest, thereby securing her future.

Between all of his wives, Black Water had thirty-five kids. And if Kenyetta acted right, he had plans to make her his eleventh. She was stronger than the others so it was harder breaking her down. He couldn't win her with promises of riches because she had her own. In order to get her, he was sure he'd have to strip her of Emerald. And if things went his way, that would be happening soon. enough

As Energy prepared his meal, Black Water palmed the back of Shannon's head in the bedroom.

"Don't forget to hold my balls, baby," he coaches.

"Sorry, daddy," she says bobbing on his dick while stroking his nuts softly.

As she went to work he thought about what he was going to do about Cameron. He always thought better during sex and with the work Shannon was putting in, he felt like Albert Einstein. If Cameron wanted to play games, he was going to write the rules. One playbook at a time.

LIL C

"I DON'T PAY A BITCH SHIT BUT AT-TENTION."

"We moved that shit already?!" Nicholas says looking more like Snoop Dog did in his prime with his hair braided. He counted his share of the weed profits from school.

Lil' C met Nicholas at Sidwell Friends, a prestigious private school in Washington D.C. It was the same school Sachi, Lani and Jona attended. The criteria was tough and the tuition was heavy but both Lil' C and Nicholas's families could afford the fee.

Nicholas's mother was a District Court judge in DC. And before meeting Lil' C, Nicholas fantasized about the Gangsta lifestyle he saw on TV. But with Lil' C, he got to live out his fantasies first hand. His privileged life was boring and he wanted a release. Lil' C used him at first because he had a car. He would've had one himself if he hadn't failed the knowledge test repeatedly. But after a while, he liked Nicholas for his loyalty.

"We knew that shit would be easy! I think we need to ask Heath for more."

"We gettin' more?"

"Yeah. I'm talking about ten thousand dollars worth."

"We ain't got enough," Nicholas says raising his eyebrows.

"We gonna ask him to front us. If he give it to us, we'll get about twenty off it. You saw how quick we moved this shit."

"Damn...if we move that, I'ma buy some pussy wit' my cut!"

"Nigga, why is you buyin', pussy? That shit don't make no sense to me!" Lil' C, says tucking some of his money under the bed, while putting the rest in his pocket. "I don't pay a bitch shit but attention."

"Come on, man. You mean to tell me you wouldn't pay fat Charlotte to fuck?"

"White girl Charlotte? Wit' the Buffy The Body ass?" Nicholas nods and smiles.

"Nigga, I already fucked that bitch!"

"No you didn't!" he responds eyes wide open.

"You don't believe me?" Lil' C says picking up his cell phone.

"Naw! You woulda told me that shit already."

"First off I don't tell niggas *every time* I fuck a bitch. I leave that shit to ya'll fools. But for the sake of clarification, watch this."

Lil' C dials Charlotte's number and waits. He places the call on speaker.

"Cameron? Is that you?"

"Yeah, shawty. How you know it was me?"

"I recognize the number." Lil' C winks at Nicholas already feeling he'd won. "Why haven't you called me? It's like you hit and ran. Did I do something wrong?"

"Naw, shawty," he says looking at Nicholas. "I just been busy. You know I couldn't forget a bad ass bitch like you. But when you gonna let me feel that again?"

"You can get this any time you want. Just say the word."

"*Word*," Cameron said coolly. She giggles.

"Aight, mami. I just wanted to hit you to let you know I've been thinkin' 'bout you. I'ma rap to you lata." When he hangs up he looks at Nicholas.

"Now what, nigga?"

"Yo, you the man for real!" Nicholas responds.

"I told you I ain't gotta do shit to impress these bitches but say my name."

"If that's true...why you bein' faithful to Lani?"

"Cause that's my Bonnie and I know when it comes down to it, she got my back."

"She seems like she don't take shit. She reminds me of your moms."

Lil' C laces up his new Gucci sneakers and thinks about what he said.

"Damn, you may be right. But I ain't tryin' to fuck my moms, nigga!"

"What?" He laughs. You takin' shit too far. I'm just sayin', Lani spunky as shit."

"Yeah...but I fucks wit' her. Sometimes I just have to shake her up cause she be violatin' my privacy. But I'ma keep her 'round though.

"You tell your peoples 'bout the baby yet?"

"Naw...I'ma rap to my pops when he scoop me up later today. And I'ma tell my mother when I get back."

"How you think they gonna take it?"

"All I know is I need to stack more paper since I got a kid on the way."

"What is you talkin' bout son? Your moms and pops *both* paid!"

"That's they money. That ain't got shit to do wit' me."

"Yeah whatever," Nicholas says picking up one of Lil' C's diamond watches that his mother bought for him. "All I know is...you livin' way better than a nigga like me."

"You lookin' at bullshit," Lil' C responds taking his watch from his hands and putting it on. "But on everything, I want in the *game* for real. I'm not tryin' to be peddlin' no bullshit at school forever. I'm tryin' to be like my pops. I want the money, power and respect. Not to mention, my mother gettin' shot fucked me up. She needs me more than she thinks she does."

"We gonna have the money, power and respect, B," Nicholas says squeezing his money stack. "If we keep fuckin' wit' them niggas from Unit B, we gonna have everything."

"That shit gonna do us good right now, but I want big money. And when it's my time...I want Emerald."

"You think your moms would let that shit happen?"

"I know she will but only when I'm ready. And I'ma prove to her that I am."

CAMERON

"THAT NIGGA JUST DON'T KNOW HOW TO HANDLE YOU."

Cameron hands the keys to his blue Mercedes CLS 500 to the valet attendant at Mercedes's luxurious high rise at the National Harbor. Taking the elevator up to her floor, he battles with his feelings for his ex. Now that he'd unleashed the beast in Black Water, he knew there was no backing out. Although years had passed since he and Mercedes ended the relationship, he still felt like she was his and was having second thoughts about killing her. When he learned she was shot, he almost lost his mind.

Once he arrives to her door, he hesitates and quietly listens.

"Please stop fussin' over me, Derrick," Mercedes says. "I'm not dying!"

Sucka ass nigga. Cameron thinks.

"Mercedes, just sit back and let me take care of you while I can. You know I have to head back to Emerald in a minute anyway."

"Well I'll be glad when you get outta here," she laughs. "You actin' like I have cancer. Is Lil' C ready yet? Cameron gonna be here in a minute to pick him back up."

"I hear you, ma. I was just kickin' it wit' Nicholas." Lil' C, says entering the room. "Should I wear my diamond watch or my Movado?"

"You already iced out wit' the chain, you should rock the Movado," Derrick says.

"You right, pop," Lil' C responds. "How you feelin' ma?"

"I'm good, son. Don't worry. It was just a flesh wound."

"I'ma fuck somebody up if they hurt you again."

"Lil' C! Don't curse around me."

"I'm a man, ma. You gotta remember that."

"Well start by learning to respect your mother, son," Derrick says.

"I know, pops, but I'm serious. What I look like lettin' somebody hurt her?"

"Lil' C, not right now. You have company," Mercedes replies.

Hearing Lil' C refer to Derrick as pop enrages Cameron and he bangs at the door.

"What the fuck?" Derrick responds as he reaches for his Glock. Walking up to the in home security monitor, he sees Cameron on the screen with an irritated look on his face. "It's Cameron," he says putting his weapon in the back of his jeans.

Derrick wants to say something negative about Cameron, but decides against it because Lil' C is present. Instead he opens the door and walks away.

"What's up, dad!" Lil' C yelled giving him a manly handshake. "Check out my Movado joint! Pop bought it for me."

The room got silent as Lil' C brought to attention what got Cameron angry.

"Did this nigga tell you to call him pop?" Although he's talking to his son, his eyes remain on Derrick.

"Naw, dad. It ain't even like that."

"Well listen...this nigga not your pops," he says pointing at Derrick. "You got one pop and that's me. I don't ever wanna hear you call another nigga pop again."

Lil' C embarrassed, looks at his friend Nicholas and then at Derrick.

"I got you, dad," he says.

"Cameron, don't act ignorant. You actin' like some jealous ass lover!"

"Aye, Cameron, I'm out," Nicholas says. "I'ma get up wit' you lada, man."

"Aight, man. I'ma hit you," Lil' C responds giving him dap.

"Lada, Big C," he says to Cameron.

"Lada, slim," he replies as he waits for him to leave. The moment he does he relives the issue. "A jealous ass lover? Fuck is you talkin' 'bout, Mercedes? I don't want my kid callin' another nigga pops. Just cause you suckin' this nigga's dick don't mean he can take my family too. Whether you believe it or not, some shit *is* off limits."

"Baby, I'ma check on things back at, Emerald. If you need me call me." He ignores Cameron. He was calm and poise and his brush off, angers Cameron further.

"Don't worry, dude. She gone be fine," Cameron affirms.

"I'm talkin' to my peoples, C. I ain't got no beef with you and I understand that Lil' C is your responsibility even though I love him like my own. But when it comes to this woman, her welfare is all mines."

Cameron smirks and says, "You can have her."

"I'll take that," he nods.

Whenever Derrick wanted to unleash on Cameron in the past, he placed himself in his shoes. It would be tough for anybody to lose a dime like Mercedes.

"Okay, pops," Mercedes says to Derrick as she places a juicy wet kiss on his lips. She was trying to get Cameron livid and it was working. "Keep me posted on Emerald."

"You got that," he winks. "Just rest up and don't worry. Lil' C I'ma get up wit' you later, homie." Cameron watches him until he disappears.

"Lil' C, go wait in the car. Let me talk to your mother for a minute."

"Aight, dad."

When he's gone he utters, "How you feelin'?"

"Cameron please," she retorts gripping the covers tightly over her body. "Like you give a fuck."

"You know I give a fuck. And why I have to hear from somebody else that you got shot? You still my kid's mother."

Mercedes looks at him and rolls her eyes. As much as she can't stand Cameron, she still has *some* feelings for him. And at one point, she was going to marry him.

"Where my daughters?"

"At my mothers."

"Good. Now stop ignorin' the question."

"I don't know why I ain't tell you," she shrugs.

"Is Emerald under control?"

"Yeah. I know you heard that some niggas ran up in City, but we met wit' everybody last night and changed the game up a little. A lot of shit is changin'."

"Like what?" he asks sitting next to her.

"You know I can't tell you that, Cameron."

The scent of his *I Am King* cologne by Sean Combs was driving her mad. He cut his curly hair down a little but it still did wonders against his chocolate skin.

"I'm your kid's father. You can tell me anything. You know I'd never betray you. I don't care what we going through."

"But you did betray me, Cameron. Remember? You let Thick convince you to dump me after you promised nothing could break our bond," her voice shakes a little as she relives the pain of his betrayal.

"You trust your fiancé?"

"Wit' my life."

"Don't make me hurt you." The room grew quiet. "How you gonna marry a nigga when you still in love wit' me?"

"W…what? Where did that come from?" She looks away briefly.

"Stop playin' games. You want me and I want you. The quicker you realize it the better off you'll be. You need me to protect you."

"How come lately you been actin' like bein' wit' you will save my life? What are you…my savior?"

"You can say that."

"Well save yourself because Derrick is the only man for me." He was about to dispute Derrick's love when she yells in pain.

"Oouuuuch!" she says holding the arm the bullet entered.

"What's wrong?" he asks touching her leg lightly.

"Nothin'…just hand me my medicine right there. And some water out the fridge." When he returns, she takes the Vicoden she got from old lady Faye and says, "Thank you, Nurse Betty."

"I'll be that," he winks.

Cameron can feel the sexual tension between them and her seductive glance encourages him. So he kisses her softly on the lips suckling her bottom one. Her stomach flutters and he runs his tongue in and out her mouth before licking the side of her neck.

"Cameron, don't make me do this. Please. Let me be happy," she begs.

"I'm gonna make you happy right now. Worry bout the other shit later."

"But Lil' C outside."

He knew he had her when her argument was no longer whether or not they should do it, but that they take care in not getting caught.

"He fine. Now let me taste that pussy again. That's all I wanna do." She tried to resist. "On everything I just want to taste you again. After that I'll leave," he says palming her breasts.

Before she can refuse, he moves the covers, lifts her nightgown and drops to his knees. He stares at her pink wet pussy. To his surprise she isn't wearing panties.

"Damn...she still pretty," he affirms licking his lips. He was about to lick her when Derrick enters his mind. Frowning he looks up at her and asks, "you been wit' him today?"

"No...he didn't wanna hurt me," she says as her legs shakes in anticipation of his warm tongue.

"That nigga just don't know how to handle you." He runs his warm tongue in and around her pussy and her familiar juices arouse him. "Damn I miss this pussy!"

As he licks her wetness, his mind wanders on their past. He remembers the look on her face when she told him she was pregnant and that it was a boy. He reflects on how she told him while making love that she would rather die than live without him. He even thinks about her smile when he bought her first candy apple red Mercedes. He misses their life together and he wants her back.

"This shit feels so good, Cameron!" she says as she selfishly enjoys his affections.

Grabbing the back of his head she grinds into his face. Cameron remembers that Mercedes never could say no to getting her pussy ate. If she had it her way, she'd choose it over fucking every time.

"Mmmmmmmmmmm! Damn, Cameron, you eatin' this pussy good as shit!" she cheers.

Suddenly tasting her isn't enough. In his mind he'd be a fool not to try to go further. If she gave him the pussy he'd know he'd have her forever. Cameron carefully lays her down to avoid hurting her arm and removes his pants and boxers. And when she's flat on her back, he eases into her slowly. A light smile spreads across his face when he notices her pussy still grips his dick. Apparently Derrick wasn't beating the pussy as hard as she claimed. Cameron was stroking her box like a first class massage therapist. And before he knows it, the look on her face shows him she's about to cum.

"Awwwww....I'm cummin' Cameron," she moans. "Don't stop I'm about to cum." When she does, Cameron releases himself into her to spite Derrick and her eyes widen. "Why didn't you pull out?"

"Cause that pussy still mine," he says.

Now guilt overcomes Mercedes and the sense of winning lifts Cameron. Silence stays between them as he returns from the bathroom with a wet cloth.

"Open up, baby," he says.

She complies and allows him to wipe his semen from her body before using the same cloth to clean himself. When he's done he puts the washcloth on the table.

Taking a deep breath he says, "Look...I know you fucked up right now, but you not supposed to be wit' that nigga anyway. It's been two years and you love me just like I love you. If it wasn't true we would not have fucked. So I'ma give you some time to break shit off wit' him before somebody gets hurt, Mercedes. Cuz I don't know how much longer I'ma let this shit go on. Hear me and hear me good...end the relationship. And I'ma call you later. Aight?"

Mercedes nods in agreement just so he would leave. She wants and needs to be alone. Cameron on the other hand, glides to his car. He knows if nothing else that her and Derrick's relationship is permanently damaged.

KENYETTA

"YOU FEELIN' THAT LIQUOR TOO MUCH TODAY!"

Yvette and I decide to walk around Emerald to see if everything is in order a week after our city was raided. And although we know they are still hiding behind our walls, we made it virtually impossible for them to make another move.

With five buildings in Emerald City and twelve floors in each of them, we created a vicious plan. There were now two armed soldiers on each floor on the opposite ends in every building. They acted as security and monitored the comings and goings of everyone. If something seemed out of line, they'd deal with it immediately. We didn't stop there. We also made sure we had two men in the front and back of every unit. Even the guard's station had two men manning the post at all times. In total, there were 150 armed men in Emerald at all times. Yeah we had shit on lock.

"So what's up wit' you, Yvette? You seem different?" I ask as we walk back to Unit C. Her hair hung down her back in a tight ponytail and she wasn't wearing earrings or makeup. She was also sporting a heavy black ski coat and baggy blue sweatpants.

Yvette looks down and drops her head. And when I look closer, I see tears streaming down her face. In all my years of knowing Yvette I saw her cry twice...once at Stacia and Dex's funeral and the other time when Thick broke her heart.

"Yeah...somethin's on my mind and I don't know how you'll take it."

"You know you can say anything to me."

Before she says anything Carissa walks up the steps and sits down next to us.

"Everything at the gate's cool. I don't care what ya'll say though. I can't stand Harold and Ed's asses," Carissa gabs. I look at her funny hoping she'd get the clue and leave but it doesn't work.

"What? Is this a private conversation or somethin'? What we keepin' secrets now?" She sips from her blue Dallas Cowboy's cup filled with vodka.

Yvette sighs and says, "I was just tellin' Kenyetta that somethin' has been on my mind lately. I'm seein' somebody who's different than anyone I've ever seen before."

"Anybody you'd be with would be different. You been with Thick all your life," Carissa responds. Lately she was drinking too much.

"Is he white?" I ask.

"No," she laughs. "I wish it was that simple though."

"Then what's up? Is he short? Fat? What?" I persist.

"He...is a she."

If I could describe the looks on me and Carissa's faces you still couldn't imagine our reactions. Carissa's cup tilts as the liquor pours out. And my mouth opens so wide, you can see my ovaries.

"Say somethin'!" Yvette yells breaking the unbearable silence.

"Y...Yvette...what you talkin' 'bout?" I stutter. "You not gay."

"Yeah, Yvette. What the fuck you sayin'?" Carissa finally says.

"You think if I had a choice I'd be in love wit' her? This shit is stressin' me out!"

"You in love?" Carissa asks with her eyes wide open.

"Yes. We been together for two years now. And since I hid her from ya'll, she cut me off. She's getting a new apartment and everything."

"Ya'll lived together too? I mean…how did you hide this from us for so long?"

"It's easy, Kenyetta. We all don't see each other when we leave Emerald."

"Damn…that's why you been dodgin' us lately?" Carissa points.

"Maybe you should put the cup down." I reply.

"Why? I'm just sayin' this explains everything to me. Your bitch ass over there lickin' pussy! Damn, Yvette! I can't believe you like women!" Carissa continues.

"I don't like *women*. I like Chris."

"So what's it like, in the bedroom?"

"Damn Car! You feelin' that liquor too much today!" I shout.

"Don't act like you don't wannna know too. We over the shock of her being wit' a woman now let's get down to the details. So start talkin' Yvette. What's it like?"

Yvette smiles a little and says, "You don't really wanna hear that shit."

"Yes we do!" I blurt out. I cover my mouth realizing I was now acting nosey.

"Now who's feelin' themselves?" Carissa laughs.

"Well, it's tender, sweet and soft."

"Girl, stop bullshitin' and get to the details! Is the sex good or not?!"

"FUCK YEAH! And don't let her strap up! Last time she fucked me wit' that rubber dick thingy I called her daddy for weeks."

"Wow! You makin' my pussy wet! She got a brother?" Carissa questions.

"Girl stop trippin'!" I laugh hitting her on the arm. "Lavelle would fuck you up!"

"That's after I get mine!"

"It's the girl who walked to you the other day? Wit' the Mohawk?" I say.

"Yes."

"She's a cutie. I see why you like her," Carissa interjects.

"What's wrong, Yvette?" I pry noticing she's crying.

"I can't believe I let her leave me! I was so happy and now she's gone!"

"You mean you let a good fuck walk out your life because of us?" Carissa adds. "Even if we didn't approve that's your life, Yvette. You don't let someone you care about leave behind no bullshit."

"Yeah, Yvette. If that's your only problem, you ain't got one."

"You sayin' that now but you called her a bitch and Carissa called her a carpet muncher!"

We all laugh again.

"We were nervous," I respond. "Look at all the shit that happened that night. And this strange person walks up to you? We were on guard."

"I know...but ya'll still said it."

"We still want you to be happy, Vette," Carissa adds. "Real talk."

"Well what about Mercedes? You heard the comments she made when she first saw Chris's face. She called her a dyke!"

"You gotta ask her, Yvette. But I think she'll recognize that real *love* is hard to find. We gonna get use to you bein' a lesbian over time."

"I'm not a lesbian."

"If you lickin' pussy you a lesbian. Fuck what you heard," Carissa clarifies.

"Anyway, Yvette," I interrupt. "If you love her, get her back. For real."

"Yeah and when you get her back ask her to lick your ass again for me. You been in a bad mood all week. Shiiiitt...if I'da known that's all you needed...I'da licked your ass a long time ago," Carissa giggles. Silence fills the air until we all burst into laughter.

"You know you went too far right?" I tell her holding my stomach due to laughing so hard. I snatched the cup from her hands. "Let me take this shit before you say somethin' else dumb tonight." I was still teasing Carissa when Yvette grows silent.

"What now, Yvette?"

"I really hope Mercedes is as cool with this as you guys are. Somethin' tells me she won't be."

MERCEDES

"I CAN BE A STONE COLD KILLER IF YOU FUCK WIT' WHAT'S MINE."

I was scheduled for duty this week in Emerald but I couldn't focus. Guilt consumed most of my waking thoughts as I replayed what happened between me and Cameron in my mind. I shoulda never had sex with him. And then he had the nerve to be acting like we were back together or somethin'. Calling my house all hours of the night! I decide tonight before going to Emerald, to deal with Cameron personally. When I knock on his door, I hear my daughters in the background playing and smile.

"Who is it?" A girl's voice calls from inside.

"Mercedes. Is Cameron here?" She opens the door, and smiles. She's tall, busty, with honey brown skin and a shoulder length haircut with a Chinese bang.

"Hi, Mercedes. Come on in. Cameron's downstairs."

I walk in and she closes the door. "You are?" I say.

"I'm, so silly," she laughs. "Your beautiful babies been keepin' me busy today. I'm Toi. Cameron's new girlfriend."

She extends her hand and I shake it. For some reason I'm not jealous that she's Cameron's new girl. Maybe it's her kindness or the fact that I want his attention taken off me that prevents me from feeling negatively.

"It's nice to meet you, Toi. Can you get him. It's kinda important."

"Girl, please! You gave that man three kids so that makes you family. Go on downstairs. He ain't doin' nothin' but runnin' his mouth with his friends. They been yappin' non-stop. Sometimes they worse than little girls," she laughs.

I laugh and say, "Okay, I'll go downstairs."

"Let me know if you want somethin' to eat. I made spaghetti."

After hugging my baby girls, I make my way to Cameron's basement. I had to give him credit, his crib in Largo, Maryland was fly. And I wonder how things would have been if we made it together. But when I think of my luxurious apartment in D.C., I smile. I have it all with Derrick.

When I reach the bottom of the stairs, I stop short when I hear two extra voices. One of the voices belong to Lavelle but the other voice I don't recognize. Wanting to hear more, I stand behind the wall that separates me from view.

"This is crazy, Cameron. They not goin' for that shit. Trust me," Lavelle says.

"They already went for it," the unfamiliar voice interjects. "That's what you don't get. Maybe ya'll handled things the wrong way last time."

"Cam, we not hurtin' for money," Lavelle responds. "We ain't gotta do this shit."

"I'm tired of this shit. Look, Cameron, if you want this dude involved you give him a cut of your money after everything is done," the other man says obviously irritated. "I'm not fuckin' wit' no scared niggas."

"Who the fuck you callin' scared?" Lavelle combats.

"Cameron, you initiated this shit not me," the stranger ignores Lavelle. "What we gonna do?" Something about their conversation scares me and I involuntarily make a sound.

"Hold up, who that?" Cameron asks.

I walk around the wall and make myself seen. Giving a nervous smile I now know who the other voice belongs to. He's Black Water from Tyland. So why was he here?

"Uh...look, man. I'm 'bout to roll. I gotta take care of some things back at the crib," Lavelle says. He walks up to me and kisses my cheek. "It was nice seein' you again, Mercedes. Bye."

"Bye, Lavelle," I reply looking at Cameron. Lavelle looks scared.

"I'm out too, man," Black responds standing up. He looks so much like Biggie Smalls it's scary. "Is it cool to leave Tamir here?"

"Yeah man...its cool."

Black exits without so much as looking or speaking to me.

"What was that about, Cameron?"

"Business. It don't have nothin' to do wit' you," he tells me walking up to me.

"So you fuckin' wit' Tyland Tower niggas? You couldn't stand them at first."

"I don't fuck wit' Tyland niggas now. I fuck wit' money."

"You know what; I don't even know why I came."

"I do. You miss me like I miss you."

"Actually I came by to tell you It won't happen again."

"Yeah okay, Mercedes."

"I'm serious! And didn't you move on with your new girlfriend upstairs?"

"What, you jealous?" he laughs.

"Nigga I have a man!" I say placing my hand on my hip.

His face frowns and he says, "She not my girl, Mercedes. You are."

"That's not what she said. I'm surprised she would even fuck wit' you."

"Why? Because she's attractive?"

"No...because she knows how to treat people. Stay the fuck outta my life, Cameron. Outside of the kids, I don't want to deal wit' you no more. I'm serious."

I have one foot on the step when he says, "You want me to murder that nigga don't you?"

Turning around I face him and say, "Don't fuck wit' my life. I'm not the dumb bitch you left in Emerald. I can be a stone cold killer if you fuck wit' what's mine. Remember that."

I walk away before he can say anything else. Heading to Emerald my mind remains on what I saw. What is Cameron doing dealing with Black Water? We use to hate his guts and now they in business together. I smell larceny. I press my Gucci boots to the gas peddle. I gotta tell my girl's I think somethin's up.

CAMERON

"I DON'T GIVE A FUCK WHO IT IS!"

"Toi, get down here!" Cameron yells upstairs after Mercedes leaves.

"Hold on baby. Let me put the plates in front of the girls."

Cameron paces the floor ready to give her a piece of his mind. He can't believe she's not smart enough to let him know Mercedes was in his house before she came downstairs. Most of all, he wonders what Mercedes heard.

"Sorry, Cameron. I fed the kids. You hungry?"

"Naw," he replies groggily.

"Okay…what's up?"

"How long was Mercedes in my house?" he questions with an attitude.

"Not long before she left…why?"

"Why would you let her downstairs, Toi?"

"Cause that's your kid's mother," she shrugs. "What's the problem?"

"Look…don't let nobody in my fuckin' house wit' out lettin' me know. I don't give a fuck who it is! She came in on a private conversation, Toi! Use your fuckin' head!" he screams.

Toi took two steps toward him, places her right hand on her hip, and smacks him in the face with her left. Turning around to leave, she doubles back and says, "Take care of your own fuckin' kids! I'm outta here!"

Stomping up the stairs, it's not long before she slams his front door. Shortly after, he hears her tires peeling out of his driveway. Cameron stands in silence thinking about what just occurred. He was feeling Toi but her aggressiveness and no nonsense attitude made him hesitate. He desired a girl like Mercedes use to be before he changed her. Sure he could've rushed upstairs and chased her down for placing her hands on him, but he'd let it past because at least she was gone. Right now he had one thing on his mind, finding out how much of his conversation with Black Water Mercedes had heard. Because he knew first hand what happened if Pitbulls attacked.

LIL C

"YOU HEARD MY WORD."

"So what you gonna do, man?" Tamir asks sitting on a chair at Lil' C's computer station. "You not gonna be able to slide out here tonight. Your pops home."

Tamir was tall, brown skin and slender with long silky hair like his mother. He kept it in a ponytail not wanting to braid or cut it. Everybody joked about how he looked just like the singer Lloyd.

Although Lil' C had only known Tamir for a few months, they hung out a few times, mainly whenever Black would come over. Although Lil' C didn't know Tamir's father as Black Water, a secret Cameron hid from him on purpose, he did know Tamir came from drug money. His pockets were as deep as his whenever they hung out. What Cameron and Lil' C didn't know was that Tamir was a spy more than anything else.

"Nigga, I'm leavin' outta here tonight. I got money to make. You comin'?"

"Naw...I know this shawty a few blocks over. I'ma check her out."

"Aight, playa...playa," Lil' C says as his phone rings for the tenth time.

"You hot as shit tonight. Tell them bitches, stop callin'," Tamir says examining Lil' C's new leather green Gucci jacket on the. Bed. "I might have to get you for this."

"You must be 'bout to leave six stacks on the table," he responds turning his attention to the caller. "Who this?"

"It's me...Jona. You busy, C?"

He looks at Tamir shakes his head and frowns. He told him earlier how she was pressing to be with him.

"Kinda...what's up wit' you though? I heard you out the hospital."

"I am, but how come you didn't come see me? It's all your girlfriend's fault," she coos in her usual high pitch baby voice.

"I know and on everything, I got into my peoples shit for stabbing you. She got into my Myspace account and saw your messages. But I gave your moms some cash for when you came back. She give it to you?"

"Yeah...thanks. I appreciate that."

As she's talking, he laces up his Nike Boots and looks in his full length mirror. Wearing a black Ed Hardy t-shirt, he can't help but smile at how good he looks.

"You wish you look like me," he says seeing Tamir placing his jacket on.

Shaking his head he decides to let him live in the jacket a few more seconds. After all, most of his friends admired his fashion sense.

"This me all day long," Tamir says. The smell of leather fills the room.

"You wish, partna." The moment Tamir removes the jacket, his t-shirt lifts in the back revealing what looks like whip wounds on his back.

"You there, C? Cause you bein' rude," Jona says.

"Hold up, J," he pauses. "Tamir...what's up wit' your back, son?!"

Tamir embarrassed, releases Lil' C's coat, pulls his shirt down and turns around.

"What you talkin' 'bout?"

Not wanting to kick his business while on the phone he says to Tamir, "I'ma holla at you in a minute." He focuses back on the call. "Look…Jona, I'm 'bout to go. Nick on his way to scoop me cause we got business in Emerald tonight."

"If you in Emerald I know you gonna stop by and see me."

"Can't do it…my girl on to us now. I ain't tryin' to hear no shit from her."

"So you gonna let her stop us from doin' what we do?"

"Like I said…I can't fuck wit' you no more. Trust me I'm fucked up cause your head game not to be fucked wit'."

"So you gonna just dump me like that?"

"You heard my word. I gotta go. Lada." When he hangs up he questions Tamir about what he saw, "Dog…who the fuck ripped your back?" Tamir is embarrassed.

"Those battle wounds. My pops makes sure we stay tough! It don't hurt no more."

He raises his t-shirt and exposes all of the scars on his back. Lil' C never seen anything so horrifying in all his life. There were about twenty or thirty deep scars on his back that rose and turned to keloids.

"I don't know about all that shit…but if your folks puttin' in work like that on you, he's fucked up, man."

"No he not! The man makes the body what the body needs to be."

"What?" Lil' C laughs.

"I said the man makes the body what the body needs to be. Not the other way around. People of the world worry too much about flesh and material bullshit. I can survive under any kind of pressure, my family too. We preparing for the bigger picture…war."

"Nigga I don't know what you talkin' about but that's some abusive ass shit right there!" Lil' C laughs. "I'ma have to get you one of them 800 numbers before your pops kills you." Lil' C eases into his Gucci jacket when he sees the head lights to Nick's Jaguar. "But on some other shit...Nick here so I'm 'bout to hit it." Tamir grabs his black and white letterman jacket.

"I'll get up wit' you, lada."

As they sneak out the garage, Tamir is consumed with jealousy as Lil' C jumps into Nick's car. Although he'd never say it out loud, what he really wanted was to be like him but Lil' C's swag was tailor made.

Months earlier, about a week after Tamir first met Lil' C, he found out from a few people in Emerald City that he was keeping time with Jona. Once he got word and a picture of her, he made sure he met Jona in a mall.

"Aye...can I holla at you for a second?" he said after walking up on her in the mall.

"You sure can cutie," she said.

By the end of that day, he had her in his bed. They had sex everyday for two weeks and Tamir bragged to everybody that he was fucking the prince of Emerald's girl.

"You know Lil' C only fuck wit' that shawty on the side right?" one of Tamir's friends said to him at a bowling party. This was seconds after he bragged how she sucked his dick moments earlier.

"Naw, that's his girlfriend." He said looking at her while she bowled.

"It ain't, man. Trust me."

Humiliated, he cut Jona off without notice and never called her again. It took weeks and a death threat from Tamir's girl cousins to finally get her to stop calling.

"I found out who he really be wit'," the same dude said a few days later. "She a twin. My cousin hang out wit' her sometimes in Emerald. I'll find out more info for you."

Tamir learned where Lani got her hair done and arranged for one of his sisters's to get her hair done that same day.

"Damn…you fine as shit," he told Lani as she sat in a chair waiting to get her hair done. Even with her hair undone she ran rings around everybody in there.

"Can we exchange…,"

"Let me stop you there. My boyfriend's a boss and I don't fuck around wit' nothin' less. You cute and everything…but I'm taken."

The entire beauty salon laughed at the way she shut him down. What she didn't know was that Tamir was relentless, and he didn't have plans to stop until he got what he wanted.

And at that time, what he wanted was her.

CARISSA

"I JUST DON'T KNOW HOW TO TELL THEM."

I was on my fourth cup of liquor and trust me when I say I hadn't drank this much in years. I don't feel safe in Emerald anymore. And I can't wait 'til it was my time to go home for a week.

We were sitting on the steps at night looking at our surroundings when Mercedes runs upstairs. I was surprised because she wasn't due back until tomorrow. And then I remember, Yvette was on the phone trying to see if Chris would come out and officially meet us tonight. It would be a mess if Mercedes ran into her.

"Hey! We all gotta talk. Now!" she says the moment she reaches the top.

"Can it wait for a minute, Mercedes?" Yvette says holding the phone. "I was about to end this call anyway."

"No you gotta hear this shit now."

"Just give me a second to get off this call. I'll make it quick," Yvette continues.

"What's up?" I ask, my voice slurring out of my control.

"Carissa, I think you need to take it easy on the liquor. You drinking nonstop. And you need to be sober for what I'm 'bout to say cause it involves you too."

"Go ahead, Mercedes," Kenyetta adds. "You making me nervous. We'll brief Yvette later when she gets off the phone."

"I think Cameron and Lavelle planning to take back Emerald wit' Black Water from Tyland Towers."

"Damn! It's my phone again," Yvette says after the phone rings a second time.

They ignore her.

"My Lavelle?" I ask.

"Yes…your Lavelle, my ex Cameron and Black Water's ugly ass from Tyland."

When she says that, I notice the look on Kenyetta's face turns to horror while Yvette steps further away to finish her call.

"Why you say that? Lavelle wouldn't do anything hurt me!"

"I was just at Cameron's tellin' him it was over, when I walked downstairs and saw Lavelle and Black Water in his basement. This not a joke, Carissa! They up to something. All of them."

"Wait a minute, I don't know where to start. The fact that you had to tell Cameron it was over or that Black was in his house. He hate that nigga's guts," I respond.

"Hold on, Mercedes. I think Yvette on the phone wit'-," Kenyetta is interrupted before she can finish.

"Let me get it out in the open. A day after I got shot, Cameron licked my pussy and fucked me in my house. So now that that's out way, can I please finish what I really came up here about?"

"Mercedes!" Yvette grips the receiver on the phone and places it behind her back.

"What?! This is serious, Yvette! It couldn't wait."

"It's Derrick," she responds. "He on the phone."

I was so drunk…I had forgotten he called moments earlier to update Yvette about the unit. Yvette, Kenyetta and Mercedes shoot me an evil glare. This is not good. It can't be.

————————————————————————————

"Lavelle, what's goin' on?" I ask him on my cell phone in the hallway. I watch my friends and know they're still mad at me. "Why you dealin' wit' Black?"

"I knew Mercedes ass was gonna start some shit. First off...you know I can't stand that nigga. That's Cam's man."

"So why were you there then?"

"Because Cam invited me on some other shit."

"I don't believe you."

"Well you should. I love you, Carissa. And I think it's time you left Emerald cause things ain't the same, baby. You got enough cash stashed away to be good and you know I got stacks. Just walk away. I'm beggin' you."

"Why though? Is somethin' 'bout to happen?"

"Baby, I been screamin' at you to leave Emerald. So don't act like what I'm sayin' to you is new."

My head drops and I say, "I *have* been thinkin' about leaving, Lavelle. I just don't know how to tell them." I look through the glass door at my friends. Mercedes is crying on Kenyetta's shoulder while Yvette rubs her back.

"For real Carissa?" he says excitedly. "You serious about leaving?"

"Yeah...I don't think I'm wanted around here no more anyway."

"Well you wanted here. I got you, Car. Come home."

"Okay. I'm ready."

"You don't know how good it feels to hear you say that shit. Don't worry about the girls. We'll think of somethin' together to tell them. I'ma call you later. I love you."

"I love you too. Bye.

I felt like a phony but I cant deny how I feel inside. I just want to be home with my man and raise our little girls, even if I means losing friends.

YVETTE

"I WOULD NEED MORE THAN HER STRENGTH TO GET ME THROUGH."

I hate leaving Mercedes while she's going through a breakup but when I called my house to invite Chris to Emerald to meet the girls, my maid told me she was busy getting the last of her things. I have to catch her before she leaves.

"Hola, Yvette. I didn't know you'd be here so early. Would you like me to prepare a meal?" Rosa, my maid asks.

"I'm fine, Rosa. Where's Chris?"

"She in the bedroom."

Rosa takes my purse and I walk briskly down the hallway to our bedroom. Her cologne freshens the halls and makes me lightheaded because I miss her so much. I slowly open the door and notice everything on the left side of the room is gone. And in our walk in closet, Chris is collecting her clothes.

"Chris," I say softly interrupting her busy body motion. She's wearing a new black Gucci sweat suit with a pair of Gucci sneaks. Damn she looks good.

She turns around and smiles, "Hey...I was just gettin' the rest of my things. I'll be out your way in a minute."

"Chris...can we talk?"

"Not right now, Yvette. I'm meetin' somebody later to let me in my apartment."

My heart drops when she says, *my* because it no longer means *ours*.

"Please. It'll only take a minute."

"There's not a lot to say," she says sitting a blue duffel bag on the bed. "I can't be who you want me to so I gotta bounce."

"I don't want us to move on without each other, Chris. I made a mistake. People make mistakes," I say walking up to her. "But you were right about me being ashamed of you and I was wrong to hide you from my friends."

"You say that but it's always the same shit." The sun hits her eyes and turns them hazel. "I'm just tired of it," she continues throwing her clothes in the bag on the bed.

"I told them about us." She doesn't stop moving. "I said I told them about us. They know everything, Chris. I told them that we live together and you're my world. There's no need in me hidin' you, anymore. I love you." My expression turns serious.

"Don't play wit' me, shawty. That shit ain't cool."

"I'm serious. They know."

"All of 'em?" she asks.

"Yes," I lie.

"Damn," she sits down. "I never thought you'd tell them."

"I did. I was a fool, but not anymore."

"What changed?"

"You left. And I'm askin' you, to please, stay wit' me. Don't leave me, Chris."

She pushes her bag out the way and sits all the way on the edge of the bed. I sit next to her needing her strength right now. Placing her hand on my knee she softly says,

"Aight. I'ma give this thing another try. But if you deny me again, I'm done, Yvette."

"It'll never happen again. I'm mad it happened the first time. I love you."

We made love until the morning. With her by my side, I can conquer the world. Little did I know, the next day I would need more than her strength to get me through.

KENYETTA

"I'M GONNA RUIN HIS LIFE FOR A CHANGE."

Entering Tyland, I locate Black's building and walk upstairs to his door without altercation. Little did he know, many of his men would kill to work for us at Emerald. Black would never be able to come into Emerald city without problems but I could.

"Who is it!?" a female calls from behind the other side of his door. I hesitate, back up and double check the apartment number. It says 316.

"Is Black here?"

A light skin female with green eyes opens the door and looks me up and down. Although pretty, she seems homely and doesn't look like the exotic types of women that Black goes for. Then again, I really don't know Black.

"How can I help you?"

"You can't help me. Does Black live here or not?"

"Yes, he lives here. Is that all you wanna know?"

Frowning I say, "Who are you?"

"I'm his wife."

Did she just say his wife? I can't believe he's married! She slams the door shut before I can say another word. Angry...I decide that Black has played so many games, that I'm gonna ruin his life for a change. Banging on the door, seconds pass before she flings it open again.

"What?!" she screams.

"Just so you know, your husband has been with other women. I just want you to know in case you think you livin' happily ever after. If I was you I'd leave his bum ass while you still can."

She laughs like she's crazy. "Shade and Shannon, come here for a minute," She holds the door open. I reach in my Gucci purse and place my hand on my Glock.

When the door widens, I see clearly inside. Although they lived in the projects, from what I could see, the inside of his apartment it was laid with expensive furniture

"Yeah, what's up?" a girl with dreads asks. The other girl stood next to her, her hair as long and silky as mine. I had to admit, they were both beautiful.

"This chick says Black been fuckin' other woman," the light skin girl says.

"Now is that so?" the one with dreads says. "By other women do you mean you?"

I remain as calm as they are and say, "Yes. I mean me."

"You must be Kenyetta," the one with the long silky hair investigates. "He told me you were a sexy little thing and I must agree with him."

She tries to touch me and I smack her hand, "You know about me?"

They laugh.

"Honey, we know *everything*," the other one says. "Black has ten wives."

"Are you bitches crazy or somethin'?"

"We taken care of," the light skin girl remarks. "Every bitch has a cheatin' man. Ours just tells us up front. It's all good."

The hallway seemed to spin. I never heard anything like this in all my life. In my confusion, I'm not surprised when Black appears from behind the women.

"I got it from here," he said taking the time to kiss all three of them in the mouth before they leave without another word. "Come in, Kenyetta. I've been expecting you. We got a lot to discuss."

CAMERON
THE SET-UP FOR THE FINALE
"I JUST WANT A PIECE OF THE PIE WHEN IT'S CUT."

In the VIP section at LUX Lounge in Washington D.C., sat Black Water, Lavelle and Cameron on large plush burgundy sofas. Opened bottles of Ace of Spade and Ciroc sat on the table in front of them while women danced sexily hoping to gain their attentions.

"Cameron, my men been in that apartment going on two weeks now." Black sips on vodka. "They got two niggas guardin' every floor makin' it hard for us to move. I keep tellin' you, we gotta push on this shit now."

"I'm ready," he says confidently. "But you never got back with me on the info about the shootin'. I tried to find out somethin' myself but came up blank."

"One of my niggas told me them dudes were from Clifton Terrace, uptown."

Lavelle shakes his head, and clears his throat at the mention of Cliffton Terrace.

"Cliffton?" Cameron repeats looking at Lavelle. "That's your territory ain't it?"

Lavelle takes a deep breath and says, "Yeah. But what happened was not my plan. Shit got fucked up."

"Damn! I gotta give you credit after all," Black Water responds with a smirk on his face. "Here I thought you was a bitch ass nigga all this time."

"I'm five seconds from breakin' your jaw," Lavelle promises.

"Whenever you get ready...I am too, lil' man," Black raises his cup.

"What you mean your plan got fucked up?" Cameron interrupts.

"I was tryin' to scare Carissa outta Emerald. I need her home wit' our daughters. So I paid these dumb ass niggas to scare her but they started shootin' for survival."

"You know they vicious wit' their aim, Lavelle. Fuck was you thinkin' 'bout by instructin' them niggas to go into Emerald? You led your soldiers astray."

"I know. It was stupid on my part."

"You know they shot my baby mother right?" Cameron holds an evil glare.

"I'm sorry, Cam. That shit fucked me up when I heard Mercedes got hit."

"Ain't you gonna have Mercedes killed anyway?" Black asks Cameron slyly.

"Naw, I just want a piece of the pie when it's cut."

"You wanted Mercedes killed?" Lavelle interrogates.

"Yeah...I mean no... I realize I was trippin'."

"Look...I don't care who lives and who dies at this point. Right now I have a vested interest in Emerald. And I need to know what we gonna do."

"I got at least twenty men who waitin' for me to take back Emerald. We ready." Cameron says.

"What 'bout you, Lavelle? How many men you got?" Black asks.

"'Bout ten."

"Well wit' the twenty men I have it brings us to about fifty."

"Okay so what's this plan?" Cameron queries as Jeezy's "Vacation" song blasts on the club's speakers.

"I say we take over Unit B first. That'll be easy because my men are already there. When I run operation "*Finale*", your men will leave their posts wherever they are even if they in Unit C. When we call, they will head to Unit B. When everybody gets there, my men will come out and flood the building. I'm not gonna lie, there's gonna be some bloodshed but after it's all said and done, we'll have what we want."

"What about the girls?" Lavelle asks.

"I suggest you find a reason to keep them away that night," Black advises. "I can't be responsible for what might happen." Although he advised them to get them out, he had plans to kill them anyway. Alive he knew they were more trouble than they were worth.

"I'll deal wit' Mercedes. She won't be there if I have to kidnap her myself."

"And I think I got, Carissa."

"I'ma give Kenyetta a warning but she might get caught up in this shit."

"Kenyetta? What you mean?" Cameron asks.

"Oh...you ain't know? I been fuckin' shawty for a minute," he laughs.

Cameron and Lavelle can't believe what they're hearing. To think that their man's Dyson ex-girl was fucking with Black, was sick.

"She didn't know who I was when we first got together, but when she found out, by that time it was too late."

"Damn...I bet the girls don't know that shit," Cameron chuckles.

"Prolly not, we might be able to use that shit to our advantage too," Black offers.

"You got this all worked out don't you?" Cameron says.

"I planned it the moment you told me what you wanted done."

"I bet," Cameron says.

"This was your idea not mine," Black reminds him.

"Once we get the building then what?" Lavelle jumps back on topic.

"When everyone takes over Unit B, Harold and Ed will let four vans inside that'll be holding twenty niggas each. They'll raid the stronger Units C and A. I hear that's where they hold the cash and product. Once we got the main units, it's a wrap."

"Unit C's security is tight. You not gonna be able to get in easy." Lavelle adds.

"I got a plan before the vans come that will help us get in. I guarantee it. I say two weeks from now we move. That'll give us enough time to brief everybody."

"What about Dreyfus?" Lavelle brings up. "I know he let you buy out Tyland but the girls turned Emerald into a goldmine. He not lettin' that shit go so easy."

"Dreyfus thinks money. If we present him with enough, he'll be fine."

"You sure about that?" Lavelle responds.

"Positive," he says. "So get ready cause ya'll about to be two of the richest niggas on earth!"

MERCEDES

"I JUST NEED TO GET AWAY NOW!"

"You want some of this?" Carissa asks holding her cup out filled with liquor.

I ignore her ass like I had the past few days.

"Mercedes, how long you gonna be mad at me?"

"This *has* gone on too long. You should at least hear her out," Kenyetta advises.

"There's nothin' to hear out. My life is some shit now and it's all her fault."

"Carissa ain't have shit to do with you fuckin' Cameron. That was all you, Mercedes."

"Oh so what? Now ya'll takin' each other's side?"

"No. I love both ya'll but the blame needs to be placed in the right place."

"And where's that?"

"On Cameron, for bringing his big dick swingin' ass 'round your house when Derrick was gone and you for being vulnerable."

I laugh for the first time since the break-up. "And how do you know it's big?"

"Don't play," Kenyetta starts. "Have you forgotten when we made a pact to take camera phone pics of Dex, Dyson, Cameron, Lavelle and Thick's dick? Cameron won!"

"He do have a fat ass dick," I agree.

Carissa laughs and I prevent myself from laughing and roll my eyes instead.

"Come on, Mercedes," Kenyetta persists. "Let's not fall apart now. Not at a time like this. We need each other now and you need us while you going through this shit."

The moment I think of forgiveness Derrick walks upstairs.

"Everything is in order. I'ma check on Unit B and I'll hit ya'll back if I find anything outta place," he looks right over my head and addresses Kenyetta and Carissa.

"Derrick, can I-,"

"Is my boss talkin' or my ex girl?" he asks interrupting my sentence.

"Your girl."

"In that case, fuck you, bitch!" he walks away and I cry uncontrollably.

"Ugh...," Carissa says out the blue.

"Ugh what?" Kenyetta asks rubbing my back.

"He sounded like a lil girl. Talkin' 'bout, '*In that case, fuck you bitch*'. Don't no man roll they head and eyes like that."

I giggle softly and wipe my tears.

"Carissa, you trippin'!" I tell her and she runs up to me and wraps her arms around my neck wreaking of alcohol.

"Oh my gawd you talked to me," she cheers rocking me like a baby.

"Yes but you have to get yourself together, Car. You're drinkin' too much!"

"I know...I know, but I have a lot of shit on my mind. Ya'll stronger than me!"

"No, we just deal with what we have to deal with." She smiles and sits down.

"I'm so glad ya'll made up. Too much shit happenin' wit' us lately. We need each other."

"You right…," I say. "So how's, Yvette? Do we know what's goin on wit' her?"

Kenyetta looks at Carissa with the, *should I tell her or not*, look.

"What? Tell me somethin' to help get my mind off Derrick.

"She dealin' wit' a female." Kenyetta says.

I'm so disgusted I almost don't respond. "Come again?"

"Yvette's been datin' this girl for two years," she continues.

"Two years! What the fuck is she thinkin' 'bout? Yvette ain't gay!"

"She is, Mercedes," Carissa says softly. "And she didn't wanna tell you 'cause she thought you wouldn't love her the same."

"That's some gross ass shit ya'll…and I hope ya'll told her 'bout herself." They remain quiet. "What did ya'll tell her?" I ask looking between them.

"We told her as long as she happy, we fine wit' it," Kenyetta tells me. "and you should be too."

"That's some bullshit, Kenyetta. Yvette ain't no fuckin' dyke! She probably needed us to set her straight and ya'll run and tell her lies. Don't forget she was wit' Thick all her life. This girl probably got up in her head because she was lonely."

"Mercedes, this ain't no fly by night bullshit. They serious 'bout each other," Carissa musters despite being drunk. "Her feelings are real and she's in love."

"WHAT THE FUCK IS GOIN' ON AROUND HERE?! I feel like I'm losin' my mind! Niggas tryin' to take Emerald, I get shot, Carissa turnin' into a drunk and you fuckin' wit' gawd knows who!" I yell pointing at Kenyetta. "Now I'm hearin' that Yvette's a lesbian and Derrick dumps me because I fucked my kid's father! I NEED

TO GET OUTTA HERE BEFORE I GO THE FUCK OFF!!!!" I scream running away.

Don't ask me where I'm going because I won't be able to tell you. I just need to get away and I need to get away now!

JONA

"YOU WANNA MAKE SOME MONEY?"

Jona sat on the floor, in the corner of her bedroom, with a cream colored phone in her hand. Everyday since she'd returned home from the hospital, she called Lil' C except today. She convinced herself she'd leave him alone but she couldn't. Blocking her number, she decides to call him again to see if he'll pick up. After two rings, he answers.

"Who this?" Loud voices play in the background.

"It's Jona...you busy?"

He breathes heavily into the phone and says, "What's wrong wit' you, shawty? Up until now I never pegged you for no stalker type bitch."

"I'm not a stalker. I just wanna talk," Still sitting, she pulls her knees toward her chest and rests her head on top of them. "Why can't we at least be friends?"

"I told you what it is, Jona. So why you buggin'?"

"Just come see me one time and I'll leave you alone. I know you in Emerald. My friends say they saw you."

"Jona...don't call me again, young. It's not a request no more."

He hangs up.

She cries softly hoping her mother doesn't hear her. But unlike the other days, now she is mad. Wiping her tears, she decides to call her crazy cousin who is staying with her uncle Hawk in Unit B. It was the same building she knew Lil' C was in.

"What's up, cuzo?" His southern accent was heavy as usual.

"Nothin'. I'ma stop by tomorrow too, before ya'll leave."

"'Cool...'cause you know we goin' back to Texas in two days right?"

"Yeah, uncle Hawk told me. Where he at?"

"Out runnin' the streets as usual. He said he was gonna bring back some grub."

"Look, Beatz, you wanna make some money?"

"You know I do. Just give me names and info." Jona got excited. "Your cousins Yuri and Gamal wit' me and gonna want in on it too. We were just sayin' we broke as shit. Uncle Hawk gives us what he can but for real it ain't shit. Is the pie large enough for all of us?"

"Yeah, but the dude you hittin' up is major. His father use to run Emerald and his mother still does."

"If he human that mean he bleed like me. So tell me where to find him."

They spent a few more moments on the phone going over the details. She told them everything she knew about the dude Lil' C copped his weed from. She told them to move quickly because he probably would be going to Lani's after he leaves Unit B and it would be harder to catch him and she made it clear that she wanted him dead.

When Lil' C rejected her, she decided that if he was going to cut her off, she didn't want him with Lani either. Without another word, Beatz woke up his brothers and got down to business.

LIL C

"I'M ABOUT THIS PAPER AND IF YOU AIN'T WIT' IT, WE CAN JUST SPLIT WAYS."

"Yo, we made out like shit! I told you that last package wasn't gonna take us no time to move." Lil' C holds a blue bag firmly packed with weed.

"Yeah…but I don't like him frontin' us this much weight," Nick warns as they walk to the elevator. "We got enough money so how come we don't buy what we can afford?"

"Cause that ain't enough for what I'm tryin' to do. This our last time because I should have enough saved for when my baby is born. I wanted this one to be big."

"What's up Lil' C," one of the Emerald City men says as they reach the elevator. Even though they all knew he was sneaking in the city, they never told Mercedes. They just looked out for him when he was there. "You out?"

"Yeah, I'ma get up wit' my girl and then I'm gone," he says entering the elevator. The soldier watches him as he waits on the elevator to make sure he get's in safely.

"I hear what you sayin' but I don't like it," Nick continues. "It don't feel smart."

"What?" he asks with a grin on his face. "You just started playin' gangsta since you been rollin' wit' me. So what you know about this shit? Everything you learned I taught you."

He hesitates and says, "This reckless, man."

"You can think what you want," Lil' C tells him. "I'm about this paper and if you ain't wit' it, we can just split ways." The elevator knocks around a little.

"Why it gotta be a problem when I say somethin' 'bout business?" he replies putting his hat back on. "I'm watchin' out for both of our backs."

"Don't worry. I got this. Just worry 'bout-," his statement is cut short.

Because the moment the elevator door opens and they step our, Beatz hits Lil' C in the face so hard, he's temporarily blinded and stumbles back. Nick rushes from behind him and does his best to help his friend. He lands a few blows on Beatz's jaw but his brothers Yuri and Gamal punish him with repeat blows to the gut. Nick's wreck game is no match for two southern brothers from the deep.

"Yo, Gamal," Beatz calls to his younger brother. "Take the package and bounce!"

Gamal rubs his knuckles and snatches the blue duffel bag. "Do you know what you doin'?" Lil' C questions standing halfway on his two feet.

Beatz laughs and says, "I know who you are and that don't mean shit to me, nigga. But you keep talkin' and I might let them pretty lips suck my dick."

Lil' C is furious and rushes Beatz with his body weight. Once he has him up against the wall, he steals him multiple times in the face. With his focus on Beatz, he doesn't see Yuri take out a knife and plunge it into Nick's gut until he yells out in pain.

The three of them stop momentarily and look at Nick as he drops to his knees. Touching his stomach, he feels his own silky blood and falls face first onto the grungy floor.

Lil' C was just about to go after Yuri until Beatz says, "Don't move, nigga." He laughs cocking the 9-millimeter in his hand. "The fun and games are over."

"Fuck ya'll want wit' me?!" he yells. "You killed my man and took my work!"

"We want your life, partna. 'Parently you got somebody real fucked up wit' you."

"Fuck you talkin' 'bout nigga?!"

"Since you gonna die anyway it don't even matter. What did you do to my cousin Jona, nigga?" Lil' C's entire body trembles. Silently he prays he'll get out of the situation alive because if he does, he'll pay her a visit. "I hope you had a nice life," Beatz raises his hand preparing to fire when four men enter the basement doorway. Three of them are carrying guns and they quickly aim at Beatz and Yuri. Lil' C knows all of them.

"Lil' C, bounce. We got it from here," Paul says with his eyes glued on Beatz. Fear washes over Yuri and Beatz as they realize they are outnumbered.

"How did you know I was here?"

"Cameron called me to come get you. Rap to him about all that when you get to the crib. We got work to do and there's a car waiting to take you home."

"What about Nick?" he asks pointing at his body.

He looked down and says, "We'll take care of everything. Go."

Before leaving, Lil' C walks up to Beatz and steals him in the face so hard his right thumb jams. He doesn't acknowledge the pain because the agony he's in is a small price to pay.

"You fucked wit' the wrong nigga," Lil' C warns. "I hope it was worth it."

With that he dodges out the door.

◀┈┈┈┈┈┈┈┈┈┈┈┈┈┈┈┈┈┈┈┈┈┈┈┈┈┈┈┈┈┈┈┈┈┈┈┈┈▶

"Don't take too long," Tony, one of Cameron's friends says to Lil' C in the car. Although he works in Emerald, he remains loyal to him. "Cameron wants me to get you out of Emerald as soon as possible. He says a lot of shit been goin' on lately."

"Just give me five minutes. I'll be right back," he promises.

Tony agrees and Lil' C jogs up the stairs and knocks on Jona's door. She unlocks and opens the door.

"What's up? I thought you couldn't come," she says nervously opening the door wider.

"I changed my mind. You not happy to see me or somethin'?"

"Yes." Although she's frightened, she hopes he doesn't know about her betrayal.

"Well are you gonna let me in?"

"Uh...sure." She opens the door wider for him to enter. Lil' C walks in without noticing that Lani sees him enter Jona's place.

"You by yourself," he asks with an evil glare on his face staring around the apartment.

"Is everything okay, Cameron?"

"Are...you...by...yourself?" he asks locking the door behind him.

"Y...yes," she stutters. "My moms on her way back though."

Not wasting time he grips her neck and pushes her against the wall. Her feet are no longer on the floor as she claws at his hands and face. His right thumb is throbbing but he doesn't release.

"They...killed my friend," he squeezes her neck tighter. Spit escapes his mouth and tears run down his face. "They killed my fuckin' friend!"

Jona continues to fight until she can't fight anymore. Small sounds escape her mouth but are not audible and her eyes roll to the back of her head. He squeezes a little tighter, releases her and watches her body fall to the floor.

"Fuckin' slut!"

With his first kill under his belt, he wipes his face with his good hand and leaves.

ED

"IT WILL WORK OUT AND IF IT DOESN'T NO ONE WILL EVER KNOW!"

Between each unit in Emerald City there was a handicap ramp between them. It was built for handicap access and led to the elevator. But most times the dope heads to shoot up in private used it. But tonight the ramp between Unit A and B would be used for a different purpose.

"There she is," Ed says as he stoops down within the ramp. "When I say go, we gotta grab her quick before somebody see us."

Kit was shaking so hard that his teeth could be heard rattling.

Kit had abandoned his post earlier to run this caper and had he not, Nick would've never gotten killed.

"I don't see her." Kit whispers

"Just wait."

Harold called Ed the moment he saw Mercedes walk away from Unit C. She was making their job easier because they had orders to kidnap her later. Black Water wanted to keep her as collateral in case Cameron reneged on their deal. And to get Harold and Ed to betray Cameron, he paid them five hundred dollars each. A small price to pay for honor.

"Go!" Ed yells as they run toward her. Mercedes recognizes his voice.

They grab her when she's not looking and pull the hood of her coat over her head forcefully. She's caught off guard because her mind was on Derrick.

"Ed? What the fuck are you doin'?!"

"Say my name again and watch what I'll do!" he promises.

"Get the fuck off me, Ed!" she screams clawing at Ed's face.

"What I tell you bitch?!" He hits her with a closed fist.

Although his duty is for Black, jealousy is his real motive right now. He hates having to report to women so he strikes her so hard in the face, her tooth falls down her throat.

"Help me bring her inside," Ed tells Kit who is so overwhelmed by how he's treating her, that he doesn't move. "Did you hear what I said? Help me get her inside!"

"I don't know 'bout this, man," Kit finally replies grabbing her arm. "This the boss. We gonna get killed if this shit don't work out."

"It will work out and if it doesn't no one will ever know!"

"How you know?"

"Cause I'll kill this bitch myself first. Now help me get her in the elevator before somebody comes lookin' for her," ED opens the basement door and they walk past the small puddle of blood in the hallway from where Nick's body was.

"Fuck happened in here?" Ed talks to himself.

"Ed please...please don't do this." Mercedes whimpers.

He doesn't answer and she wishes she had enough strength to fight but she doesn't. She's in so much pain that her head throbs uncontrollably. When the elevator opens, they rush her inside. When it moves, Ed grabs his phone and calls the person assisting him on the fourth floor. Like the other units there were two soldiers on each post so they had to get rid of the other one.

"Yodi, we on our way up," Ed says as he eyes Mercedes lustfully. He can't wait to be inside of her. "Get rid of that nigga."

"Got it," he tells him.

"Yo, Peanut," Yodi says after placing his phone in his pocket. "Somebody just called and said they need you downstairs. They said Kenyetta wants you."

"Why Kenyetta ain't call me?"

"'I don't know 'bout all that but you betta check it out."

"I'm not supposed to leave post."

"Let me call him back and tell him you said fuck, Kenyetta." Yodi pretends to be dialing out.

"I'm goin'!" he yells stopping him.

Against his instinct, Peanut leaves his post and heads for the elevator on his side of the floor. It was the opposite end of the direction Ed and Kit were coming in.

"He gone," Yodi says calling him back. "But hurry up before he comes back."

"We comin' now." He lifts Mercedes up who was helplessly lying against the railing. "We got to get this bitch in Harold's crib quick. And I don't know 'bout you, but I'ma hit this shit before I go back on post. I wanna see what boss pussy be like."

MERCEDES

"WHEN I WAS YOUNGER I DIDN'T BE-LIEVE IN HELL."

I can't believe this is happening to me. I'm actually being kidnapped by Ed and taken into Harold's apartment. Carissa told me she never trusted them and I wish I would've listened. And the way I left saying I just needed to get away, I doubt if they try to find me anytime soon.

"Is that who I think it is?" someone says when we enter.

"Yeah...," Ed boasts closing and locking the door. "This one of them."

A bunch of men I don't know circle me and feel my body. I fight back tears.

"Back up niggas," Ed laughs. "I know ya'll been stuck in here forever but whatever ya'll plannin' gotta wait. Me and Kit caught the fish so we get to eat it first."

"I'm fine, man," Kit says shaking his head. "You go 'head."

"Suit yourself." He removes the gun from his coat and strikes the back of my head with the handle for no reason. He follows up wit' another blow across my face which slits my eye and blood rushes inside of it. "I'm fuckin' this bitch until I can't fuck her no more."

I fall to my knees and he drags me by my hair to the bathroom. My body brushes up against empty pizza boxes, beer cans and trash all over the floor.

"This nigga actin' like a caveman and shit! Don't bash her up to bad!" Someone says. "I want her pretty when I get to her."

"Fuck you, nigga, before I make her off guard to ya'll funky bastards."

They laugh and Ed opens the door and throws my body across the edge of the tub. The cold porcelain presses against my stomach. He roughly removes my coat and pulls my jeans to my ankles. Almost naked, he tugs at my panties until they tear apart.

"Ed, we been good to you," I say softly. "And if you let me go, I won't tell anyone about this. I'm the mother of Cameron's kids."

The moment I say Cameron's name he pushes his dick inside of me hard. "Please...," I sob. "You're hurting me!" He violently grabs my hair, pulls it backward and licks my face.

"Bitch, all this was Cameron's idea anyway. You callin' that nigga's name ain't doin' shit but making me hard. So shut the fuck up before I get *real* violent."

He slams my head foreword and it bounces off the inside of the tub. More of my blood exits my body and goes down the drain. For twenty minutes he rapes me until he can't rape me no more. And one after the other, men enter the bathroom and then my body. I counted about twenty men after Ed left me. Some were gentle while others were rough, nasty and rude. But after the third one, I became numb. There was no more crying and no more begging them to stop. I needed to preserve my energy.

After they were done...hours passed and the rapes stopped. They carried on conversation like I wasn't there. In between shitting and pissing in the bathroom, they'd talk to me like I was trash. One of them made me open my mouth while he pissed inside of it. I threw up for an hour until he got tired of hearing me gag and threatened to kill me.

When I was younger I didn't believe in hell. I thought it was a place old people talked about to keep you in line. I was wrong. Because there's no way you can't tell me that I'm not in hell…on earth…right now.

LIL C

"I SHOULDA KNOWN YOU WAS FOUL!"

Lying on his bed in the dark, Lil' C was still battling with the lost of his closest friend, Nick. To make matters worse, his father wouldn't tell him what was done with Nick's body or his car. The moment Lil' C got home that night, Cameron stopped him from telling anybody he was the last one with him.

The first day, Lil' C hated his father for making him lie to Nick's mother. It was difficult to hear her cry, begging him for any details. Just when he thought things couldn't get any worse, he discovered his mother had been missing for days. Lil' C was taking things hard.

"You ready to talk now?" Cameron asks. He turns on the lights in his room and plops down on the edge of his bed.

Lil' C, laying flat on his back with his hands behind his head and his legs crossed briefly acknowledges his father. "Not really."

"Well we gotta talk anyway, C. Now I know you're hurtin' but what's done is done. You wanted in the life now here it is." Lil' C nods. "So how does it feel?"

"How does what feel?" Lil' C turns to look at him.

"Your first kill?" Lil' C is shocked by his statement. "I know everything. One of the soldiers saw you enter that youngin's apartment the night her mother found her murdered. Don't worry 'bout it. They told me and we took care of everything."

"I don't know how it feels. I mean...the first night I kept seeing her face. So I stayed up that whole night. Now I'm fine. I just can't get over Nick. He was tryin' to protect me and they killed him. They had what they wanted, so why didn't they just let us go?"

"That's the game, son. You wanted to be a man and this is how it is. The rules are heavy and if you gonna be in this lifestyle, get ready. Everybody's a target."

"You know 'bout the drugs too?"

"I know everything you do, C. I sent my man to scoop you up from unit D the moment I found out you snuck out of here. Usually I let you be because I know you growin' up and wanna be with your friends...but not this time. I'ma tell you the truth, I ain't know shit 'bout them niggas 'bout to rob you. They out of town-ers and right now anybody not from the city got the spotlight on 'em. So when they passed one of the soldiers at the elevator, and said your name in conversation, my man called me right away. I called Paul and had him shoot over there. Sounds like he got there just in time."

"Not really...they still got Nick," Lil' C says in a low voice.

"I know, but they ain't got my son. But look, C, you gotta stay away from Emerald. Shit is heavy."

"I ain't scared of no niggas! I go hard!"

"I'm not askin'," he said with a scowl. "You gotta stay the FUCK out of Emerald. And wit' your mom's gone, I wanna keep an eye on you to make sure you're safe. She don't need to be stressin' when she come back. Understood?"

"Yes."

"Good...don't make me catch a body for somebody hurtin' my only son."

"Where you think ma go?"

"I don't know. People sayin' she needed to be alone."

"You think she gonna come back?"

"I think she will. Everybody need to escape sometimes."

Lil' C takes a deep breath and says, "Dad...I gotta rap to you 'bout somethin'." Cameron nods for him to proceed. "Lani pregnant."

"How, man?" He's upset. "I get you a pack of rubbers every time I get mine."

"I know, but she my main shawty. It just happened."

Cameron shakes his head. "How you know it's yours, C? These young bitches be runnin' game out here."

"I can't really explain it...I just know."

"Well you know what that mean don't you? You gotta do right by your seed."

"I plan to. That's what I been grindin' for."

"You ain't gotta grind, C. You know we got you."

"I'm a man, dad. I gotta take care of my own seed. How I look like gettin' money from my peoples for my kid?"

Cameron smiles at his son and says, "You're right. How come she hasn't called?"

"I don't know. We ain't talked since Nick died. I just wanted to be alone."

It wasn't until then that Lil' C realizes that she hadn't called him.

"Aight...but look, I settled your bill on that package you copped from the kid in Unit B. And we caught up wit' Hawk, broke a few legs and made him tell us where his nephews rest in Texas. I'ma send somebody up there to take care of him next week. He sold it for half of what is was worth to some niggas on Kennedy Street before he left."

"Thanks, dad. I got you later on that."

"I know, next week you work for me. This way I can keep an eye on you."

Lil' C nods and Cameron leaves the room. Picking up the phone, he calls Lani.

"What's up, Cameron?" she says dryly.

"Look...before you get started I know you mad at me for not calling you. I been goin' through some shit and needed to be alone," he pauses. "So I been...-,"

"What do you want, Cameron? I got company so right now I'm busy."

"Company? What you talkin' 'bout?"

"I understand you been gone a while, but it sounds like you still know English," she says sarcastically. "So let me spell it out, I have C.O.M.P.A.N.Y. And since you like to fuck my friends, I decided to try yours," she giggles and Lil' C feels his blood boil.

"So you fuckin' other niggas now? That's how you carryin' it?"

"We DONE, C. So get over it, cause I'm already over you."

Lil' C pumps himself up to unleash on her and says, "You know what, it don't even matter to me. Just as long as that nigga, whoever he is, stays away from my baby when he's born."

Lani laughs and says, "Boy I had an abortion yesterday. Trust when I say you free to go on with your life, boo, boo."

She gets off the phone and someone says, "I'ma need you to stop callin' here. I wasn't tryin' to get in ya'll's business but you still on the phone, dude."

Tamir's voice enrages C.

"I shoulda known you was foul!" Tamir laughs. "So you fuckin' my girl?" he barks.

"Naw...I'm fuckin' *my* girl."

Lil' C tries to understand how he even knew her. Although he rapped to him about Jona, he never talked about Lani because he respected their relationship around his friends. Taking two deep breaths he decides not to let anymore of his feelings show.

"You can have that slut, but don't let me catch you on the streets, playa."

"Don't worry, homie. Our time will come."

"Indeed."

Tamir hangs up the phone and Lil' C decides to make another call. "Is Monie Blow home?" he asks the woman who answers.

"Who the fuck is this?"

"Lil' C. A friend of hers."

The phone drops and the woman yells, "Monie, get this fuckin' phone! I told you I don't want nobody callin' my house!"

"Ma, shut the fuck up!" she says picking up the phone. "Who dis?"

"It's C. From Emerald."

"Oh, hey C," she says in a nice voice. "I'm glad you called 'cause I ain't think you liked me. You know, wit you bein' from Emerald and all."

"I fucks wit' you. That's why I'm callin'. You know Lani and Sachi jumped your cousin right." He says hating how petty he sounds.

"I know…that bitch betta neva let me catch her."

"She said she waitin' on you. I just wanted you to know. Be careful."

"Waitin' on me! I'm from Tyland T all day! We don't play that shit! Wait till I tell my girls! It's gonna be on!"

C got off the phone with her and lies back in his bed. He knew Monie and her girls would handle Lani and he had plans for Tamir. He couldn't predict how many men he'd kill in the future, nor did he know their names. But he was certain that before he left this earth, Tamir would be put to rest, by his own hands.

YVETTE

"YOU AND ME TOGETHER WOULD'VE BURNED THIS CITY DOWN."

"Kick that mothafucka in!!!" I tell one of the four men with me.

Boom! Crash! Crash! When the door comes down, a lady feeding her infant quickly jumps up and hides her breasts.

"Run through this mothafucka and tell me if Mercedes in here," I look at the frightened mother. "Don't worry. If she ain't in here we'll be out in a second."

As I await their word, my hand remains on my weapon. I'll kill this bitch if I have to. Ever since I heard the way Mercedes left, I felt uneasy. Upset or not she wouldn't leave us like this.

"She ain't in here, boss," Carson says walking out.

"Fuck!" I look at the woman and her child. "Look, I'm sorry."

"I...I understand," she stutters. "I really hope you find her."

"For a lot of people's sake I hope we do too."

Carson gives her some money for the repairs and we move to the next apartment. We must've kicked down twenty doors with no signs of Mercedes yet. I'm losin' it!

"Kick it in," I instruct them at the next apartment.

When the door swings open, I see a man I always talk to inside. I use to give him his props for taking care of his daughter alone. And here this nasty mothafucka was, sittin' on the couch and making his ten year old daughter suck his dick!

"What the fuck?!" I scream.

"Fuck is this dude doin'?" Carson asks enraged at the sight.

I don't have to tell them what to do next because all four of my men stomp him until he's motionless. I hold his daughter back with my hands so she won't get hurt.

"You okay, baby?" I ask.

"Ye...yes," she says shaking.

"Where's your mother?"

"Locked up."

"Why?"

"She stabbed him for hurting me."

Dirty bastard. "Look, put some clothes on. I'ma take you to the lady's next door."

She trots in the room and gets dressed and we take her to the lady next door.

"Don't worry. I'll take care of her," she smiles. "Go find your friend."

We were just about to knock down another door when Carson says, "Boss, I don't think she in this building. I think we should try Unit B."

"Why? Somebody said the last time they saw her she was over here."

"Somethin' seems weird about unit B lately. I remember walkin' up on two dudes the other day and when they saw me comin' they stopped talkin'."

"And?"

"Well...the night Mercedes was shot, Harold came 'round back when I was on post. He was actin' funny and seemed weird. It always stuck wit' me. He said he was on his way to his crib when he *happened* to see my ride fucked up. I'm tellin' you, boss, I think he got me to leave my post on purpose. I know it wasn't the same night Mercedes left, but I think them niggas in that buildin' up to somethin'!"

"Harold, huh? Carissa said repeatedly that she didn't trust them."

"Yeah...I *really* don't trust him or Ed. And somebody said the night Mercedes left, that Ed wasn't on post. Said he was gone for 'bout thirty minutes."

My breaths are quick and I try to slow them down. I'm on the verge of a panic attack. I had to plan a better raid. We could go over Unit B to kick down doors but that could backfire. I'm gonna have to play it smart .

"Look, when I tell you to, I want you to bring Ed to me, tonight."

"What you want me to say?"

"Tell 'em we tryin' to find Mercedes and we havin' a meetin' with only the people we trust. I'll take care of the rest."

"Got it."

"Gimme a hour. I have to set a few things up and I'll call you."

"Okay. And I'm sorry I ain't tell you earlier, boss. I guess I thought he was just slackin' and it wasn't a big deal."

"Never wait to tell me somethin' again, Carson. Trust your instincts. Always."

"I won't. It'll never happen again."

◄┈┈┈┈┈┈┈┈┈┈┈┈┈┈┈┈┈┈┈┈┈┈┈┈┈┈┈┈┈┈┈┈┈┈►

"Why you leave without me?" Kenyetta asks when I run up the stairs. "You can't be on a mission alone. What if somethin' would've happened to you?"

"I wasn't alone, Kenyetta. But I gotta find, Mercedes." I look at her worried face. "Okay, Kenyetta, I'll be more careful, but I gotta plan to find her that I think will work."

"What is it?"

"I think she's here. In Emerald. So we're gonna hold a meeting with our most trusted men. Somethin' in my blood tellin' me some shit is goin' on, especially after Mercedes said Cameron and Black were together. I think Mercedes missing and that meeting with Cameron and Black are all tied together."

"Damn...so what you want me to do?" Kenyetta asks.

"I want you to invite twenty people you trust and Carissa you invite twenty," Carissa was so quiet I forgot she was here. Her face was in her cup. "If you can't trust them fully, don't invite them. You wit' me, Carissa?"

"I can't do this," she says under her breath. "I'm tired of being afraid."

"So you wanna abandon us? At a time like this?" Kenyetta responds.

"I just wanna raise my kids wit' 'Velle. I don't want any of the money."

"Money? Fuck you talkin' about."

"This not me no more, Kenyetta."

"I can't believe this shit!" Kenyetta screams.

"Please don't be mad at me," she cries. "I'm still your friend. Please!"

"A friend? Who abandons?"" Kenyetta responds. "No such thing."

"Let her go," I say gently touching Kenyetta's arm. "Just let her go."

Kenyetta looks at me and shakes her head. "Whateva happened to the pact we made? Right after Thick dumped you? We said nobody could break our bond. So why are you leavin at a time like this. What about Mercedes, Carissa?! She needs us."

"It's over, Kenyetta. If she wants out we have to let her go." Kenyetta walks away and down the stairs. I grab my phone and call Carson. "Look, keep an eye on Kenyetta. She just left Unit C upset. Make sure nobody hurts her."

"I got it, boss."

After the call I think about Carissa. I saw the breakdown in her eyes a while ago.

"You free to leave, Carissa," I smile. She gets up and hugs me and I hug her back.

Before leaving she tells me, "I love you. I love all of you."

"I know you do. Now go take care of yourself."

When she leaves, I see Derrick rushing up the stairs. His eyes are bloodshot red.

"Why you ain't tell me, Yvette?!!" he yells. "Why you ain't tell me Mercedes been missin' all this time?"

"Calm down!" I say with my arms out in front of me, so he couldn't approach me. "I didn't tell you cause you and me together would've burned this city down. But don't worry. I got another plan. We gonna find her, Derrick. Trust me."

CARSON

"MUST BE NICE TO BE SO RELAXED."

The weather was cold but the stars shine brightly on the field of Emerald city. Carson found Kenyetta and Yvette was thankful. She then had him go get Ed.

Carson walks toward the guard station where Harold and Ed are standing post. But before reaching them, he approaches two soldiers who are a few feet from the gate. He considers them cool because the girls hired them all and they got their chances together. Most of the other soldiers were hired on Cameron's watch.

"What up, B?" Carson says to one of them before giving him a manly handshake.

"Ain't shit, shawty," Dipbug says. "The city on high alert! Niggas noid as shit around here!"

"I feel you," he confirms. "What 'bout you, Kit? You holdin' up?"

Carson wasn't saying it, but what he was trying to do was feel them out.

"I'm good. I just be glad when shit gets back to normal around here."

Carson took note at how fidgety he was.

"No doubt. You 'aight, though?" Carson asks Kit. "You lookin' kinda nervous."

"I'm good. It's just cold as shit out here."

"I feel you. Look...I gotta holla at Ed right quick. I'll get up 'wit ya'll later."

"Everything cool?" Kit asks.

"I don't know…is it?" Kit doesn't respond. "I'm just fuckin' wit you. I'll get up wit' you later." He made mental notes to tell Yvette that something was up with Kit too.

"Aight, man," Dipbug says.

Carson walks toward Ed and Harold who were playing cards in the booth. "Must be nice to be so relaxed. Considering the city is on high alert."

"It is nice," Harold replies. "So why you not on post?"

"'Cause I'm on some otha shit tonight," He smirks. "Ed, let me holla at you."

"What up?" Ed asks before looking at Harold. "I was 'bout to crush this nigga in this game."

"I gotta rap to you *now,* homie…and we got to do it alone."

"Aight," he relents. When they are alone he says, "What's up?"

"Look man, Yvette holdin' a private meetin' wit' the people she trust. So everybody ain't invited on this one."

"She trusts me?" he points to himself.

"Why? She shouldn't?"

"Fuck yeah!" he says cockily. "Yvette know I got her back."

"Cool, we need you to come right now. We tryin' to find Mercedes."

"Oh, aight. Let me tell Harold."

"Man, we have to leave now. If she wanted Harold to be in on it, I would've told him myself. We gotta roll now," Carson demands. "Harold gonna be aight. Dipbug and Kit got him."

Carson could tell Ed was guilty. Not only were they too lax at the gate to be in the middle of a war, but his vibe was foul. Both of them. And if the opportunity presented itself, he'd be the first to take them out.

ED

"IF I CAN DO ANYTHING TO HELP, COUNT ME IN."

Ed and Carson walked to community center. There were ten rooms inside and Ed was led to the one on the far end of the building. Ed's instincts told him something wasn't right. But what could he do? Once inside the room, he saw Derrick sitting behind a desk.

"What's goin' on, man?" Ed asks him. "Where's Yvette?"

"She comin'. For now you need to sit back." Ed sits. "You aight?"

Ed swallows hard. "I'm cool. I just wanna do my part to find Mercedes."

"Is that so? Tell me, if you were gonna find her, where would be the first place you'd look?"

Derrick gets up and sits on the edge of a table across from him.

"I don't know. But I'm fucked up about her missin' like you."

"Fucked up about her missin' like me?" Derrick points to himself. "Naw, my dude. You could never be as fucked up about it as me. Neva."

"You know what I mean. If I can do anything to help, count me in."

"Oh I know you will help me find her," Derrick smirks. "I'm sure of it."

Ed's phone vibrates indicating he has a text message. The message says, '*In twenty minutes we movin'. Be ready.*' It was from Harold.

Looking up at Derrick, his expression shows guilt.

"That was my, man," he says trying to erase the message.

Carson snatches the phone and reads it. "Fuck does this mean?" He asks him. He doesn't respond. "Derrick look at this shit!"

Derrick takes the phone, reads the message and looks at Ed with an inquisitive stare.

"You got two minutes to tell me somethin' before I start pushin' your teeth down your throat."

He stands over top of him.

Ed spends the next hour explaining what he can about the message, softening his involvement in everything. He hoped what he was willing to say, would be enough.

It wasn't.

YVETTE

"YEARS AGO WE FOUGHT TO KEEP EMERALD. AND WE WON."

I look around the conference room in the community center and see 56 men we feel we can trust. They all wait on my word.

"As you all know Mercedes is missin'. And we think whoever came through our gates had something to do with it. We also think they're still here. We called you all here because we need your help finding her and we know all of you are loyal to Emerald. We have to look out for one another during these times. Things are about to get serious," I say.

"Can I say somethin'?" Kenyetta asks walking up to front.

"Sure," I respond backing away so she can take the floor.

"This is war, fellas. Years ago we fought to keep Emerald. And we won. We are fighting a new war today, and we'll win again. There will be bloodshed and lives may be lost. But we promise, if you ride wit' us, you'll all benefit for your sacrifices. Can we-,"

Before Kenyetta can finish, Derrick busts through the community center door.

"I gotta talk to you," he says interrupting the meeting.

"Excuse us for a minute," Derrick says. We all take a few steps back. And the men in the meeting talk quietly amongst themselves as they wait.

"We got Ed," he whispers. "And he told us they plannin' to take down the city tonight." Derrick is anxious. "Black Water and Cameron are involved."

I see Kenyetta stumble a bit and I help her keep her balance, "You aight?"

"Yeah…yeah I'm good," She stands on her own two feet. "Go 'head, Derrick."

"They're sendin' texts to everybody involved in their plan. Whoever with them will receive a text and walk off no matter where they are to meet in Unit B. I ain't sure, Vette, but I gotta strong feelin' my shawty in there too. That nigga stuck to his guns 'bout not knowin' shit about where she at but I know he lyin'. Cameron involved."

"I just can't see Cameron bein' involved in kidnappin' her," I say.

"If he ain't involved, it sure looks like it," Derricks responds.

"The boy Cameron never learns," Kenyetta says. "He fucked up! He needs to move on!"

"I know," Derrick adds. "Looks like he's gonna need my help."

While we are talking, one of the men in the front row looks at his phone and walks toward the door. Me, Derrick and Kenyetta look at each other.

"What's goin' on, Vick?" Keneytta says to the man *she* invited to the meeting.

"I just gotta check on my post right quick. I'll be back."

"Well *we* tellin' you its fine. So they can wait," Kenyetta told him. "Nothin's more important than finding Mercedes."

"It can't wait," he continues moving toward the door. "I'll get up wit' ya'll later."

He was almost at the door when I yell, "Somebody drop his ass!"

A few men move to do it but Doctanian, one of our oldest friends, enters the door and knocks Vick out. He was coming in as Vick was going out. I called him earlier to tell him what was happening but couldn't reach him so I left a message. Apparently he came straight over after hearing it. And although he owns a sports bar outside of Emerald City now, and was no longer in the drug game, he's still considered family.

Rubbing his knuckles from laying Vick out he says, "Who is this nigga?"

"Somebody who got exactly what he deserved! Dropped!" I tell him.

Doctanian laughs and walks up to us. We embrace and already feel safer with him around.

"I heard about what happened, so I dropped everything and came through. Whateva you need me to do, I'm in!" Derrick gives him a handshake and pulls him in a one arm hug.

"Thanks, man! For comin'."

"Please. You was there for me when Erick killed my shawty and dumped her."

The thought of the same fate happening to Mercedes sicken our stomachs.

"And I'm here for ya'll I don't give a fuck who we gotta murder! We fam!" Doctanian continues.

We talked a few more seconds alone, and reconvened our meeting. Shit was about to get real serious in Emerald. Guaranteed.

BLACK WATER

"BY THE TIME THEY MAKE A MOVE IT'LL BE TOO LATE."

Black was watching his sons' fire at empty beer bottles in the back of Tyland Towers parking lot. His sons ranging from 16 to 19 crashed each bottle with a single shot. Although young, they were marksmen. And at present, no man or woman in their age range or older could fuck with their firing skills. Black Water had been training them since they were old enough to hold a weapon. His other sons ranging from 10 to 13 were waiting to fire at the targets next. Because tonight it would be them, not their older brothers who would get a chance to show their skills. In the entire world, there was not a group of children more vicious or coldblooded than the children of the Black Water Clan.

"What you mean you can't find Ed?" Black asks as his younger sons finally step up to practice. He's on his phone. "When was the last time you saw him?"

"When Carson came to get him. I don't know what was said because they stepped off. But the way Carson looked at me, made me feel like somethin' was up." Harold says. "They may know something."

"You could tell all that by a look?"

"That and one by one dudes started leavin' post and shit. I asked a few of 'em what was up, but they ignored me. They knew something I didn't."

"It don't matter. By the time they make a move it'll be too late."

When Black's call ends, he watches his wives Shade and Shannon walk toward him with their guns in hand.

"Ya'll ready," he asks kissing them on the lips.

"We were born ready daddy," Shade says wrapping her arm around his waist. "So don't worry, we got you. Everything gonna go smooth."

"It better." He says.

HAROLD

"PEOPLE HAD CHOSEN THEIR SIDES AND NOW IT WAS TIME FOR BATTLE."

"Okay it's 'bout to be on," Harold says when he enters his apartment. The men had recently got off of the phone with Black and knew now was the time to move. "I just spoke to Black and our troops are movin' toward this building as we speak. I doubt very seriously all of us gonna make it outta this shit alive though. So if you wanna get some pussy from that slut in the bathroom you betta do it in now, cause it might be your last fuck in life."

A few of the men line up next to the bathroom door preparing to rape Mercedes again. Harold had raped her earlier that day and wasn't interested anymore.

As he looks out of the window, he wonders what was to become of him. He was frightened.

There was not a soul on the field. People had chosen their sides and now it was time for battle. He wonders if the women they called Pitbulls were as vicious at he'd heard or if it was just a rumor. Either way, he realizes it is too late to turn back now.

MERCEDES

"IF I'M GONNA DIE I'M GONNA DIE LIKE THIS!"

I don't know what happened but I *snapped*. I grew tired of the sexual abuse. Fifteen men raped me today and I was raw and in pain. No longer could I just bend over and *take it* like they told me over and over again.

Don't ask me where the strength came from 'cause I can't be sure. Maybe it was the food Kit snuck me every-day when everyone else was asleep. Or maybe it was thinkin' about my children being left with Cameron. Whatever it was, caused me to grab the last man who was about to climb on top of me, and choke him until the life left his body.

"Fucccccck youuuuuuu!" I scream. I'm naked from the waist down.

Spit escapes my mouth and drops on his face. I'm in a murderous rage. If I'm gonna die, It'll be fighting. I squeezed his throat so hard, my entire body trembled. When he stops fighting, I place my head on his chest, but my hands remain on his throat.

"Mothafucka!" I say out loud squeezing his throat one last time.

When I'm sure he's dead, I take his weapon, and re-move his jeans. They're too big for me but will do for now. Once dressed, I grab the 9 and open the bathroom door.

The weapon shakes and I tell myself if someone tries to stop me, I'm pushing his wig back.

I heard them earlier saying a war was getting ready to take place in Emerald and I need to be there for my friends. For my family. Easing out of the bathroom, I notice everyone is gone and I hate the apartment, which held me hostage for so long.

Barefoot, I tiptoe toward past the living room and to the front door. I stop myself from opening the door right away. I hear their voices...in the hallway. Suddenly I'm scared. What if they catch me? Fuck it! If I'm gonna die, I'm gonna die fighting! There was just no way I could give up. Pressing my ear against the door, I listen attentively.

"That nigga betta hurry up and come on," someone says.

"He probably in there makin' love and shit," another one says.

They laugh.

Judging on how close they sound, I gage they're about a few feet from the door. Taking one deep breath, I open it and run into the hallway. The gun in my hands shake at I aim at them in whipping motions from side to side. My hair's all over my head and I'm nervous. The oversized jeans I'm wearing fall down a little exposing my vagina. And I focus on Kit, the man who nursed me through the toughest experience in my life.

"Get your hands up!" They slowly comply as I pull up my pants. "K...Kit...get the fuck outta here!"

He looks at me.

"Go, Kit! Now!"

He carefully runs down the stairwell.

"I knew I ain't trust that nigga!" Harold says.

"Shut the fuck up!" I yell. "Don't make me shoot one of you mothafuckas!" I scream backing up slowly. I caught them off guard so they couldn't pull their weapons when I first entered the hallway. "Stay still or I'll shoot anybody who makes the slightest move! I'm not fuckin' playin!"

They remain still and I continue to back up toward the elevator. I press the button with my free hand. Someone moves and I fire hitting him in the chest.

"I'm not fuckin' playin! Don't make a fuckin' move or I'll shoot all of you niggas one by one! Keep your hands in the air!"

They remain like Toy soldiers. And the moment the elevator door opens, I jump inside. When the door closes someone says, 'Get that bitch!' And my heart races.

Sweat runs down my forehead as I nervously stand in the elevator, my bare feet stick to the filthy elevator floor. If they run down the stairs before this door opens, I'm dead. I hit the basement button several more times trying to hurry it along.

"God, please help me. Please." I say trembling.

Once the door opens, I run out of it and away from the building. I hear their voices behind me. Their footsteps pressing against the grainy dirt grow closer but I'm barefoot and fighting for my life. I can't let them catch me. I won't let them catch me.

"I'ma kill you, bitch!"

"Fuucckkk you!" I say.

They are many but the gap between us grows larger. I'm too fast! I was fighting for my life. It's hard to catch a person who's running for her life. My feet appear to grow wheels as I run faster and faster.

"Yvette! Help Me!" I scream into the field.

I wonder where everyone is but I'm relieved I don't hear anyone behind me anymore. They're all gone! Thank God they're all GONE!

I run to the community center because we made a pact a long time ago, that if one of us ever got in trouble, someone would always be at the community center to receive him or her if they could just get there. The plan was made when Dex and Stacey were alive and we prayed we'd never have to use it. But I needed this plan to work for me right now.

Once there, I push open the double doors and my bare feet make a squishy sound. Quietly I walk toward the door where we hold our meetings and twist the knob. It's dim inside but I see someone on their knees praying. I walk closer aiming my gun and the person stands.

"Derrick?" I ask shaking terribly. I smell his cologne and know it's him.

"Baby," He walks up to me and takes my weapon. Placing it on the table he says, "Is that really you?"

He examines my bruised face, messy hair and over-sized jeans. "You so beautiful. You're alive and you're so beautiful!"

I fall into his arms and he holds me tightly. For the first time in days I'm home. In his arms I'm really home.

CARISSA

"FOR THE MOMENT I NEED TO BE COMFORTED."

I can't believe I'm free from Emerald. And up until a few weeks ago, I never realized I wanted to leave. Luckily for me I had a man who loved me no matter what.

"What you thinkin' 'bout, baby?" Lavelle asks as he runs his fingers through my hair. We're stretched out on the couch watching Keyshia Cole's TV show that I record-ed.

"I'm just happy to be here wit' you that's all."

"You just sayin' that," he jokes. "You ain't tryin' to be wit' a nigga for real."

"I *am* happy," I look up at him. "Had it not been for you, I probably would've gotten killed in Emerald. I'm tired of having to look over my shoulders all the time."

"I don't know what I would've done if somethin' happened to you. But you ain't gotta worry 'bout shit now. I got you...I got us."

"I know...I just don't wanna lose my friends. They like my sisters."

"They should love you know matter what. And didn't you say Yvette understood?"

"She did but Kenyetta didn't and Mercedes still hasn't come back yet."

"You can't worry 'bout them. Your focus should be on me, and our family."

"That's easy for you to say. You and Cameron still cool. You have your friends, I don't."

"We are cool but for real we not."

"What's that supposed to mean?"

"Nothin," he says rubbing my face. "Shit just not the same wit me and Cam. For real shit ain't been the same since we left Emerald. Don't get me wrong, Cam gonna always be my nigga. We just don't see eye to eye on everything anymore."

"Me and my friends are like that too." I laugh remembering our beefs. "But I got you so for real, I don't care."

"Yeah, well if that's true, how come it don't seem like it?"

"I'm sorry, baby. It's just that a lot of shit kicked off in the past few weeks."

"There you go worryin' about that Emerald city bullshit again. You a woman not a man. So stop trying to do man's work."

"Lavelle you sound selfish. I mean...why wouldn't I care about my friends?"

"It ain't selfish!" he yells. "I'm tired of you worryin' 'bout shit that don't concern you. To be honest you might as well get use to the idea that as long as they stay in Emerald, somethin' *will* happen. Be grateful you got out in time."

I sit up and look into his eyes. I feel he's trying to tell me something but I don't know what. So I scoot next to him and say, "What you mean?" He takes a deep breath and briefly looks away from me. I pause Keyshia's show and can feel my heart racing.

"I'ma be real wit' you. Emerald about to fall, and that's why I wanted you out."

"Emerald about to fall? You act like you know some-thin'."

"I do," he says seriously. "Cameron plannin' to take it back."

"Take it back?" I remember Mercedes talking about Cameron, Lavelle and Black being together, but when I asked him was something up, he said no. He even threat-ened to end our relationship if I asked him again. "Fuck you talkin' about, Lavelle?"

"In the next few days, Black from Tyland and Came-ron runnin' up in Emerald. And when they do, they not plannin' on leavin' without the money and the city."

"La...La...Lavelle," I can't catch my breath and I feel betrayed. "When I asked you was something up you told me no. I trusted you. Why did you lie to me?"

"Because I did what I had to do to get you out. That's why."

"Please explain to me what you're talking about." I stand and place my hands on my hips.

He looks down at the floor, stands up and walks up to me. "I'ma tell you this 'cause I don't want you to hear it from nobody else," he says placing his hands on my shoul-ders. "I had somethin' to do wit' them dudes who ran up in Emerald blastin'."

"The ones who killed the guard?"

"Naw. The ones who shot Mercedes." I smack La-velle and his mouth bleeds.

"I deserved that, but you know I never meant to hurt you and if I had to, I'd do it all again. I love you."

"You love me? You don't love me! It's cuz of you, Mercedes got shot. What if she would've gotten killed?"

"I know I fucked up, Car. But they wasn't supposed to shoot ya'll. I paid them to scare you a little and that was it. I guess they got nervous and felt like they lives were on the line. But just so you know, your girl, Kenyetta guilty too. She been fuckin' around wit' Black behind ya'll's back."

"Stop lyin', bastard!" I yell.

"I'm serious! He got a thing for black women with that Indian look and Kenyetta is it."

"Why should I believe you?"

"Because I'm your man. Now I'm sorry baby," he pulls me into his arms. "But I was worried about you. Can't you understand that? Come here. Let's not do this. Okay?"

I don't respond and fall into his embrace. For the moment I need to be comforted. And had he walked away, I'm not certain that my limp body wouldn't drop to the floor. I know its wrong…and I may even seem disloyal, but for the moment I need him.

LAVELLE

"SO WHAT SHE PLANNIN' TO DO WIT' ME?"

Lavelle slept hard after making love to Carissa for two hours straight. When he woke, he couldn't get over the sensation of feeling drugged. A smile crept across his face when Carissa told him that despite his lies, she'd still stay by his side. Waking up, he turns around preparing to go another round. But when he touches the sheets, he notices her side is cold and she's gone.

"Carissa!" he yells thinking she was preparing breakfast. "Get back in the bed. I'm tryin' to get some mornin' pussy."

"She gone, man," a soldier from Emerald says.

When he looks in the direction of the voice, he sees two men inside of his bedroom sitting in chairs. He recognizes both of them.

"But she asked us to be here when you woke up," he continues.

Lavelle reaches for his weapon under his pillow. It's gone. He reaches for the nightstand. It's not there either.

"It's not there, dude," one of them says. "And if you get outta line, we got orders to slump you."

Lavelle sits up and leans against the bedpost. His bare back is cold against the wood. With everything going on, he laughs to himself because he didn't see this move coming along. Carissa was smarter than he thought.

"She went to Emerald?" he asks.

"Yeah…man."

"So what she plannin' to do wit' me?"

"We don't know yet. But the moment we find out, we'll show you."

YVETTE

"THEN LET'S GET READY FOR WAR!"

After the meeting we exit through the back door and the sight of fifty men outside temporarily stops my heart. We didn't invite them so what did they want? Were they with the others?

"I know ya'll not tryin' to do this shit right here," I look at the men. "Cause I can guarantee you if it goes down like this, a lot of bodies droppin'. So what ya'll wanna do?!"

"We not here for that, Yvette. The city is divided. Some went to Unit B and we're here to fight wit' you. Everybody talkin' about a war and we wanna make sure we on the right side," Smiths says, his young face was sliced in six different directions.

"Yeah, we ain't 'bout to let them niggas just run up in here and take our shit!"

I'm not too sure I can trust them. But when I look into their eyes, I feel they're being true and we needed their help. The more the better.

I smile, walk up to them and say, "Then let's get ready for war!"

We told them as quickly as possible what they needed to know about our plan. Leaders were picked. I take twenty with me and we head to Unit B. And after our session was over, we split up in groups to cover various parts of the city.

"Ya'll ready for this shit?!" I yell at my twenty men.

"Fuck yeah!" they cheer.

"Then let's drop these niggas and show them the mistake they made for violatin' our city!" Weapons clank in the air.

As we walk on the field toward Unit B, I notice everything is quiet. Not one soul was outside, not even tenants. Word travels fast so I'm sure they're staying clear of drama. They know what's getting ready to happen.

"Yvette, I think it's finally happenin'," Kenyetta says looking around. "We really going to war. We really have to fight for what's ours."

"You think," I say playfully. "I've never seen the city like this before. It's a ghost town."

"I'm so ready for this shit, though," she says excitedly.

"Good 'cause they not gettin' Emerald unless they take my life with it."

"They betta take mine too," she responds touching my hand.

As we walk toward the back of Unit B, I hear a voice calling my name. My men immediately cover us.

"Yvette, it's me! Mercedes!" She runs toward us and the men part.

She moves toward us and my body shivers. My friend. My best friend, is here. And I thank God for answering my prayers.

"Oh my God...She's alive, Vette!" Kenyetta screams.

We run toward her, meet in the middle and embrace. She's alive!

"You don't know how good it feels to see you," I say holding her face in my hands. "Do you know what I was about to do?"

"'Bout to do?" she laughs. Her face is bruised and she limps. "I heard you were in Unit C kickin' down doors and shit!" We all laugh. "I'm just happy to be back."

"Where were you?"

"Let's talk about it later," she says as sadness washes over her face. "But thanks for remembering the plan to have someone waiting in the community center."

"You know I would never forget something like that."

She smiles and squeezes my hand. "Thank you. Hey...where's Carissa?"

"It's a long story," Kenyetta tells her.

"So what's the plan now?" Derrick asks bringing us back to the present and our reality that the war was far from over.

Kenyetta, Mercedes, Derrick and I continue our walk toward Unit B. Our men walk behind us.

"Most of our men are guarding Unit C because the cash and product is there. But we're hitting Unit B first because we know they're inside. Two men will guard each of the eight floors and two will guard the back in case anybody tries to get in or out. Two more men will also watch the front and they'll also keep watch on the yard. The set up will be pretty much the same for all units.

"We have to break down their inside crew first and than prepare for the takeover later tonight. Now on one of the floors in Unit B we already have two men inside. They reached out to us earlier and told us they were going undercover. Black doesn't know about them and thinks they're with them. But on our command they'll do what's necessary. Once we're in position, we're gonna take over two apartments on each floor that'll allow us to see the yard clearly. That way we can cover all bases in case someone tries to come on the grounds."

"What about the gate?" Mercedes asks.

"It ain't safe. So our men on the roof will kill anybody who tries to enter."

"It sounds solid," Kenyetta says nodding her head. "I think it'll work."

The look on Derrick face tells me he thinks otherwise.

"What's up, Derrick. Are we missin' somethin?"

"I'm not sure, but somethin' not right. I mean, why would they flood Emerald and stay in Unit B? The money and shit in C."

"It's hard to get in Unit C. They had to get into the weakest unit."

"Naw," he disagrees. "Somethin's up. Somethin's not right."

"We got to do somethin', D. We have to move."

Derrick takes a deep breath, still visibly uneasy and says, "Then let's do it."

◄┄┄┄┄┄┄┄┄┄┄┄┄┄┄┄┄┄┄┄┄┄┄┄┄┄┄┄┄┄┄►

IN A UNIT B APARTMENT

"They're here. Tell Black," Harold says to Tamir on the phone.

"Why you ain't call him?"

"I did...but he ain't answerin' his phone. So he told me whenever I couldn't reach him, to hit you."

"Aight...I'll get him the message."

"There's somethin' else, the girl Mercedes got away."

Tamir laughs and says, "He not gonna be happy wit' that, but I'll let him know. Just hit me back if anything changes," Tamir stresses. Harold doesn't like taking orders from a kid but something tells him if he works for Black, eventually he'd have to deal with him anyway. "And Harold...don't fuck up again 'cause in our family losers die."

MERCEDES

"I HOPE MY JUDGMENT ISN'T CLOUDED"

My body's sore but I don't tell them. I want the focus to be on Emerald City and not on me. I focus on the field in front of me. When my phone vibrates with a blocked number, I decide to answer.

"Who is this?"

"Ms. Mercedes, it's me. Lani."

"Lani, why are you calling me and why are you blocking your number?"

"Because I thought you wouldn't answer."

"What do you want?"

"To speak to C. He won't talk to me. And I need to talk to him."

"Lani I spoke to C earlier today and he told me you got with his friend so your problem is your own."

"Please, Ms. Mercedes, his friend beat me and I broke up with him."

"Lani, now is not the time. Lil' C's got a lot going on and so do I. So don't call me anymore."

After I end the call I try to reach Cameron again but he doesn't answer. He's avoiding me but eventually we'll speak, whether he wants to or not. I know he had everything to do with the rape and that hurts me.

Thoughts of what I did to Ed run through my mind and made me smile. Derrick gave me the pleasure of killing him and I did it slowly. I wrapped my hands around his throat and squeezed as tightly as possible until he was gone. I didn't take my eyes off of him until the Vanishers removed his body.

Now standing at the bottom of Unit B's steps, I watch the gate and the yard. Kenyetta is at the top of the stairs watching me. And I was growing sick of her asking if I was okay.

"You okay, Mercedes?"

I turn around, look up at her and say, "I'm cool."

"Who was on the phone earlier? You look angry."

"It was Lil' C. He been at it since I been gone. When I talked to him earlier he said he got somebody pregnant, she aborted the baby and than got with his friend."

"Lil' C having sex?"

"I know. It's gross right?"

"I don't want to think about it anymore."

It was silent until light gunfire sounds off in Unit B and I worry about Yvette and my squad. I look up at Kenyetta who says, "Yvette and Derrick gonna be fine. Trust me."

"I know, it's just that...," before I finish five kids come running from the gate through the yard.

"Help! Help!" the children cry fanning their arms. "They gonna kill us! Please!"

They were carrying backpacks, and were barefoot. From where I stood they look to be between the ages of ten and thirteen. Loud and hysterical, their pleas for help were the only sounds on the quiet field.

"What you want us to do, boss?" one of the soldiers asks from one of the apartment windows in Unit A. His gun was aimed in their direction. After his question I hear multiple weapons clicking although hidden from view.

"Hold fast," I tell everyone with my hands up. "Don't do nothin' yet. They just kids." Turning around I say, "Stay there, Kenyetta. I'ma check this shit out."

"Don't go by yourself," she says worriedly. "I can't see you clearly over there."

"I'ma take Keith from Unit A with me," I say jogging toward the gate. "You just stay here in case Yvette calls. And watch my back."

"You know I got you! Be careful!"

"Keith, come with me," I holler.

"I'm on it!" he says running behind me.

On the way there, I see the children are followed by two women. The women look scared and both have complexions like Kenyetta's. To be honest, the three of them look like they could be sisters. I notice one of the two women is carrying a gray hobo style purse and her feet are bare. The other is wearing slippers.

"Fuck are ya'll doing in Emerald?" I ask them.

Keith's weapon is drawn.

"Please...you gotta to help us," the woman with the dreads says.

"I ain't gotta do shit, bitch! But you betta tell me somethin' I wanna hear and quick before you have a situation to deal wit' right here!" When I see her holding a purse tightly I say, "Take her purse, Keith and look through that shit." While he's looking I say, "Now what's goin' on?"

"Someone wants us dead. And we're responsible for these kids. Trust me when I say we had nowhere else to run. This was the quickest place we could get to on foot."

"Where do you live?"

"In Tyland Towers," she says softly.

Keith looks at me. His eyes say what I'm thinking. *This is a set up.* But the children were confusing me. Either they were good actors or they were really scared.

"I know this looks crazy. But we run a day and night children care center. Their mothers had *just* dropped them off when my boyfriend who works for Black told me he was goin' to have anybody who had family in Emerald city murdered. My cousin lives here and he knows it. You don't know it but Black, he's crazy," she sobs.

As we speak the children continue to cry remaining huddled against the women.

"When we found out," the other woman says who had long silky hair like Kenyetta's. "We came runnin' over here."

"Ya'll don't have a car?" Keith asks.

"Yeah...but we don't have enough space for all the kids," she replies.

"What about the parents?" I question.

"We didn't have time to call," the one in the dreads says. "When my boyfriend called and said Black had some people on the way up, we had to move."

"Please help us," one of the kids says grabbing my leg. "I want my mommy."

"Get off of her," Keith tells the child.

"It's fine," I tell him. "They just babies."

"Boss, I'm not tryin' to disrespect you, but this don't feel right."

"I got it," I assure him. "I got it."

I look down at one of the boys and he reminds me of Lil' C when he was younger. Suddenly I feel bad for them. After all, I'd just escaped a near death situation and would've wanted someone to help me. I hope my judgment isn't clouded because of it.

"Can you help us?" the woman with the dreads repeats. She looks behind her once more in fear. "I'm worried if we stay out in the open, they'll kills us. I'm beggin' you."

"Which unit does your family live in?" I ask.

"Unit C. I have her number if you want me to call her," she continues.

Reaching in my pocket I pull out my phone. She gives me the number and the moment I hear a squeaky voice I know who it is. A Troublemaker.

"Keri, it's me, Mercedes. Somebody's out here for you. What's your name?"

"Whitney," the one with the dreads replies. "I'm her cousin and this is LeLe."

"She says she your cousin Whitney and some chick name LeLe wit' her too. You know them?"

"Yeah," she says without hesitation. "Are they okay?"

Still not sure if this was real or not I said, "Describe her."

"She's real pretty and she wears dreads."

I knew even if Keri was looking out the window, where we were, she couldn't see them clearly. Anyway, her window faces the backside of the building. I quickly make up my mind to save the children.

"She on her way up. This betta not be no bullshit, Keri or I'm comin' for you," I say hanging up on her. "What's up with the bag?" I ask Keith.

"It's clean. The only thing she got in here is a tampon and a bag of M&M's," he continues tearing the edge of the bag and eating the candy.

"Aight," I say looking the women up and down. "You can take the kids upstairs."

Something in my spirit tells me I'm making a bad decision. All of them were about to walk away until I say, "One of ya'll stayin' wit' me."

"O...okay," the one with the dreads stutters.

"You with the dreads stay with me. I wanna keep ya'll separated."

"But Keri's my cousin," she complains.

"Stay wit' me or get the fuck outta Emerald. It don't make me no never mind." I lied.

If she didn't take my offer, and I found out later something happened to these children I'd feel some kind of way. But true to my word, if she didn't listen, all of these mothafuckas would have to get off of our grounds.

"Okay," she says putting her head down. "I'll go with you."

"I'm stayin' wit' you too," the shortest child says holding onto her leg.

"Is it okay?" she asks looking down at him and then up at me.

"Whatever, just come on before I change my mind."

"Boss you want me to look in them backpacks before they go inside?" Keith asks.

"Hold up!" I yell stopping everyone from walking toward the building. "What they got in them bags?"

"We don't know. Their parents bring them everyday when they drop them off. We told them to grab what they could before we left. You're welcome to look inside," Lele replies.

I look at the kids and remember how Lil' C was when he was younger. I made a point that whenever I needed a sitter, she would have to stay at my house just so my kids could be around their things.

"Let 'em go" I turn to the men in front of Unit C. "They goin' up to Keri's! Let 'em inside and tell whoever's guarding the floor to call me when they get there!"

"Got it!" one of them responds. As we walk up the stairs to Unit B a nagging voice in my head yells, "You're making a mistake!"

The only thing was, it was too late.

KENYETTA

"I WAS IN LOVE"

When Mercedes walks up the steps with someone from the gate, for a moment, I think she's lost her mind. At first the night sky conceals the person from view but I soon recognize her. She's one of Black's wives. I met her at his place, but what is she doing here?

"What the fuck is she doin' here?" I ask Mercedes when they reach the top.

"Don't worry. I got it. Black was on some bullshit in Tyland and they had to hide out here. I'll figure things out later."

As Mercedes speaks, the bitch smirks at me. She knows I didn't tell her about Black and she's using it against me.

"Let me take them inside," Mercedes says. "and then we'll talk."

The moment they attempt to pass me to walk to the door, I lose all sense of reason. Taking out my gun, I aim...pull the trigger and hit her in the head. Guts and blood from her body hit the dirty glass window and my face.

"Oh my, Gawd, Kenyetta!" Mercedes screams holding her mouth. She was bloody too.

When I'm sure she's dead, I aim at the child but Mercedes jumps in front of him.

"Fuck are you doin'?" Mercedes asked, placing the child behind her. "Whatever's goin' on you know I got you, but I can't let you shoot no kid!"

"Are ya'll okay over there?" one of our men yell from another unit.

"You need us?" another one calls.

"Uh…yeah, everything's cool!" I reply.

I look at Unit B hoping Yvette would be out soon. I just want this over with and I never thought I'd have to do what I was about to…tell one of my closest friends that I betrayed her.

"Kenyetta what the fuck is up?!" she screams again, the child looking around her and up at me. I wasn't sure, but something told me he had deadly plans.

"Please don't hurt me, Miss lady. I'm just a kid," the child cries.

When I *really* look at the boy's face I feel sad. What have I become?

"I'm sorry, Mercedes. I'm losin' my mind right now, but I got to talk to you," I told her putting my weapon up, the dead body still at our feet. "Jones, can you keep him in the hallway with you?" I ask one of our soldiers inside the building, who was guarding the first floor. "I'ma have somebody take him up to Fat NayNay's later."

"No problem, Kenyetta," he says nervously. "I got lil man."

When the child steps over the dead body, my heart breaks. It feels like we were living in Afghanistan instead of in our Nations capital. We were becoming so use to murder that it wasn't phasing us anymore. We place a quick call to the Vanishers and I prepare myself to be honest with my friend.

I take a deep breath.

"Mercedes, I got to talk to you."

"Go 'head," she responds anxiously. "Cause you got me fucked up right now."

"I…ummm, use to date Black."

"Black who?"

"Black Water. From Tyland."

"I'm not understanding what you're tellin' me."

"You know Dyson never use to let me leave the house when he was alive. It was like I was his slave. If I wasn't with ya'll, I couldn't go anywhere else. I was his little Indian girl," I laugh realizing how stupid I was back then. "I felt like I was in hell sometimes because he would leave for days and when he came back, he did not want to be with me. It was just me and my worrisome ass grandmother all day in that apartment by ourselves. I was bored and hated life."

I look and pause.

She says, "Go head, Kenyetta. I'm listening."

I exhale. "Well because I never got out, I never saw Black's face. I heard of him but never saw him. And when we finally met, he didn't tell me who he was at first. A year passed before he finally told me. By that time I knew I should've dumped him, but I didn't. I was in love."

"Damn, Kenyetta," she says shaking her head. "That's some heavy shit."

"I know," I cry wiping a tear from my face. "I know it's fucked up, but that's not all. He wanted me to have a baby and I was so wrapped up in having a man that I brought him on Emerald city's grounds to have sex. He was testing my loyalty to him and I fell for it."

"What?!"

"I'm sorry. I violated our bond and our sisterhood and I was wrong."

"The Vanishers here!" a man calls breaking our conversation. "Let them in?"

We look at the black beaten van coming through the gate and I say, "Let em come through."

Although no one was guarding the gate from the station, our men still had intentions on shooting to kill. Our conversation pauses as the Vanishers walk up the stairs, pick up the body and remove it from the grounds. As usual, they never ask us questions and we never volunteer. Just as long as their direct deposit is sent to an offshore account monthly, all is good. Ng did a good job of keeping our secret.

When they were gone just as quickly as they came, I look at Mercedes. "I'm sorry about this shit. I really am."

"Did you help them niggas come in here? The ones who killed Jake?"

"No! I swear! I knew nothing about that! I let Black Water in once felt bad, and never saw him again."

She exhales and says, "I'm not gonna lie, this shit is fucked up, Kenyetta. But...but...I know you love us and I understand how it is to be wrapped up in some bullshit. I just fucked a man who didn't deserve me and almost lost a man who did."

"So who was she? That girl you killed."

"His wife," I say shaking my head. "That nigga got ten of them. I can't believe the shit this nigga's on. He had the nerve to ask me if I wanted to be his eleventh wife. He's crazy!"

"You didn't know he was into that shit?"

"Fuck no! You know we never really talked about Black. The only time we mentioned his name was when we heard that they were tryin' to steal our customers some years back. It was when Critter was alive. I never knew he was a bigamist!"

"Yeah...he been wifin' chicks for years! Damn, Kenyetta, I never realized how clueless you really were."

"I know." I smile. "Dyson was my life."

"You got any other secrets I should know about?"

I take a deep breath and say, "Yes. I had sex with Dex before he and Stacey were killed. I was at my lowest. I know it was wrong but I had to tell somebody because it's been eating me up alive."

Mercedes looks away and says, "I already know."

I gasp.

"You know?"

"Yeah, she told us. She said he told her what happened between you two. He said you were about to take your life. She was hurt, but she loved you enough to keep the friendship and not cause you any pain by bringing it up."

"Dex told Stacey we made love?"

"Yeah. I didn't think you'd ever tell us, especially after they died because the secret went with them. But, Stacey cried for days after Dex told her and when she was done, she put it out of her mind. I don't know if you remember her sitting with us one day when we were on the steps at Unit C."

"She sat with us all the time."

"I know, but this time she sat close to you and told you she loved you. She told you that nothing could ever break ya'll's bond. Stacey knew you weren't trying to steal him from her. And she never held it against you."

"I can't believe it," I say.

"I know but in her mind it was *us* before them. If she had to choose between you and Dex, it would've been you. Trust me, if Dex didn't get her out of Emerald like our no good ass niggas back then, she would've rode with us to the death."

Wow. I would've never thought Stacey would've handled it the way she did. She was a real solider! And I would forever look up to her after hearing this. Had one of my friends fucked my man, I don't know how I would've reacted. On second thought, I probably would've handled it like she did. I guess it speaks to our friendship. We had a bond that was unbreakable.

We were still talking when Yvette came running out the front door.

"We found some of 'em," she says breathing heavily. "Most of them were in apartments spread out on the second floor. We killed eight of them already. They weren't in Harold's crib though, Mercedes."

"I figured," she says.

"Doctanian and Derrick are watching the floor right now. We gonna have the men knock on a few more doors so we can get the rest of 'em. And then we goin' in blazing."

"We only have twenty somethin' men here. If we all go upstairs, the front and back doors won't be secured.

"I know. But we still got the men guarding the yard in the other units. They'll let us know if anybody comes in or out of here. But we got to move. This shit got to stop tonight. We need to reclaim what's ours."

CAMERON

"IT AIN'T ABOUT HOW MANY GOONS YOU GOT, IT'S HOW YOU USE 'EM"

"You comin' or what?" Black asks as he sits in the back of his silver chauffeured stretch Hummer. "Tonight's the night. We movin' on Emerald."

Cameron and he met in the parking lot of Eastover Shopping Center on the borderline of DC and Maryland.

Cameron takes a look at the limo and says, "This a bit much ain't it?" He places his hands in his pockets and steps back to get a better view.

"If you got it, it ain't. This how ballers roll."

Cameron laughs and says, "I bet. But look, there's been a change of plans."

"You sure it's not a change of heart?"

"You can call it what you want." He says stepping closer. "I tried to call you to tell you I ain't fuckin' wit' it, but you ain't answer your phone," Cameron says nonchalantly.

Black pats his pants realizing he left his phone on the bed at his house. He'd taken it off right before making love to his three wives.

"Aight...well I missed the call. So what that mean...you bailin' out now?"

"First off get out of the car and talk to me like a man. I ain't some bitch you tryin' to hook up wit'."

Black laughs, and exits the car. His height, size and build makes him seem more powerful than Cameron believes he really is. But one look in Cameron's eyes, you knew that he was more powerful.

"Now what?" Black barks.

"Like I said, I'm not fuckin' wit' it. It's done. Shit has gone too far already."

Black Water shakes his head in disgust and breathes out heavily.

"I knew you was gonna pull some shit like this," he laughs. "That's why I had that whore baby mother of yours kidnapped for collateral. Don't you get it Cameron? Shit ain't over till I say it is."

"I think you missin' an update," Cameron replies in a sinister tone. "And you betta be glad I don't smoke your bitch ass right now."

"And update?"

"Yeah, she got away. I taught her good."

The smile is wiped from Black's face and his lips press tightly together. He's in a furor.

"You know you betta never step foot on Emerald city grounds again right?"

"You just betta hope I don't find a reason to."

"Is that so?"

"That's so...and you can forget about my niggas helpin' you in Emerald. They behind the girls now. You on your own, partna. Good luck," he chuckles.

"Do you really think I'ma let Mercedes live once Emerald is mine?"

"I don't think about it either which way. All I know is what's done is done and at this point, I'm sure she could hold her own."

Black looks toward Cameron's car parked a few feet over from his. A girl was inside.

"I see why you not trippin'." Cameron looks back at Toi who is impatiently waiting and he smile smiles.

"Naw, I ain't trippin' cause I don't give a fuck."

"Well...I guess we said all we need to. For your sake I hope our paths don't cross again. I got niggas everywhere," Black says pointing behind him. There are five vans parked behind Black's car. "Remember that."

"It ain't about how many goons you got, it's how you use 'em," Cameron replies.

He points at Black's jacket. Black follows his stare and sees a red dot on his leather coat.

"You got it," he says nervously not knowing where Cameron's gunman was located. "For now anyway."

"I got it always," Cameron replies. Black gets in his car and it drives off.

When Cameron steps back in the car, he braces himself to deal with Toi. He knew she was mad after sitting in the car for thirty minutes waiting on him.

"Are we goin' to the Luxe or not? I'm ready to get a drink and party."

"Give me a kiss first," he says. "And stop being so damn mean. You gonna make your face ugly." Toi laughs and they're lips meet.

"You betta watch the people you hang around. Everyone not in your corner, Cameron."

"Toi, mind your business. It's over anyway. I got it."

"We'll see."

EMERALD CITY SOLDIER
"I'M TWO SECONDS FROM TAKIN' CARE OF THAT ATTITUDE PROBLEM FOR YOU."

Twenty year old Wallace was leaning against the wall watching the first floor. In the game for only two years, Wallace had visions of moving up the ladder and becoming a lieutenant. He worked tirelessly around the clock and often got by with less than three hours of sleep. He lived and breathed Emerald and the girls noticed. He was well on his way.

The kid who was left with him, sat on the bottom step after Yvette and the others went upstairs. The little boy spent most of the time in his book bag and seemed to be preoccupied with its contents.

"What you got in that bag, man?" Wallace asks playfully. "You been in that mothafucka for five minutes straight."

"Why?" the kid questions in a smart tone. He looks him dead in his eyes as he waits for his response. "I didn't ask you what you got in that whack ass coat you wearin' so why you all in mine?"

To be ten Wallace was caught off by his attitude. Earlier he seemed timid and scared. Now something in his eyes told Wallace everything he did was an act.

"You got a smart ass mouth to be a lil' youngin'," Wallace tells him standing up straight. "You betta watch that shit though. You might find yourself in a situation you can't get out of."

"Nigga fuck you. I ain't gotta watch shit! If some-body got a problem wit' me they can suck my dick."

Wallace was about to break on him until he took into consideration the murder he witnessed earlier. He figured seeing the death was causing his brash tone.

"Was that your moms who got hit earlier?"

"No. She was my aunt. Why?"

"Hey, shorty, I'm two seconds from takin' care of that attitude problem for you. So how 'bout we do this, don't talk to me until it's time to roll and I won't say shit to you."

"How 'bout I just shut you up permanently," the child says standing up, his arms behind his back.

"Lil' nigga you trippin'…" Wallace's statement was cut short by a bullet entering his body.

The sound of the gun firing was quieted by a silencer. But Wallace was hit in the shoulder and had he not moved a little when he saw the gun, it would've entered his heart instead. His body fell against the bronze mailboxes as he slid to the floor.

"What the fuck," he says touching the wound, his fingers were wet with his own blood.

He needed access to his weapon in his coat but knew if he moved, the kid would fire again.

"I see you ain't sayin' shit now," the kid smiles walking up to him. "You should learn not to talk so much cause you never know who you talkin' to."

The boy was preparing to shoot again when Chris opens the building door, knocking the little boy to the floor with a blow to his face.

"What the fuck is goin' on?" she says rubbing her knuckles staring down at the child. "Kids killin' niggas and shit!"

"I don't know who you are," Wallace says to her. "But I'm sure glad you came through when you did. That lil' mothafucka was about to smoke my ass and shit."

"It looks like he already did."

Chris was only there because she was looking for Yvette and heard she was in Unit B. When she saw the little boy holding a gun and approaching Wallace, she thought her eyes were playing tricks on her. But the closer she got to them the surer she became. A child was definitely about the kill a man.

"I sure hope you on the right side of this shit 'round here," she says stooping down to look at his bullet wound. "Cause I might have to finish you off myself."

"I should be askin' you the same thing," he responds trying to avoid showing his pain.

"Is there somebody I can call for you? You losin' a lot of blood."

"Yeah...my phone in my pocket. Just redial the last number."

Chris grabs his phone and makes the call, both of them keep their eyes on the unconscious boy.

"What's up Wallace? Everything cool?" a female asks.

"This ain't Wallace," she says standing up. "This Chris, he been shot."

"Who the fuck are you and what you talkin' 'bout?"

"Your man is lying on the floor and he losin' a lot of blood. He needs help."

Mercedes got silent for a minute before saying, "How do I know this ain't a set up?"

"Hold on," she stoops back down and places the phone to Wallace's ear. "She wanna talk to you."

"Mercedes, I don't know who this is but she just saved my life," he says as the phone rests on his shoulder. "But I'm real fucked up right now. I need some help."

"Aight, I'll be down in a moment. Just hold tight."

It took Mercedes two minutes to get downstairs and she brought her soldiers Lando and Neo with her.

"What happened?" she asks Wallace as the men help him up.

"I don't know. I was about to check the lil' nigga for his attitude and the next thing I know he starts shootin and shit'. I think it had somethin' to do wit' Kenyetta smokin' his peoples."

"Damn," Mercedes says briefly assessing the situation. "Keith said lettin' them fuckin' kids in without checkin' they bags was a mistake," she pauses and grabs her phone. Calling Keri, who she believe was involved, she's disgusted when she doesn't answer. "Look, Neo, take my man to Old Lady Faye's to get him fixed up and then find out where them kids in Unit C at. I think somethin's up." Neo helps Wallace up.

"What about the kid?" Lando asks.

"Take him to the community center after yall drop Wallace off and don't let this lil nigga out of your sight. Guard him wit your life."

"Got it boss!" they say as Neo lifts the child from the floor.

"Now what the fuck are you doing here? And how did you get past my men?"

"I was here before everything went down. I been stayin' at my friend Davida's and her man's crib in Unit A."

"So how you find us?"

"Somebody told me she saw her outside a little while ago. Look...I ain't tryin' to start no shit cause I can see a lot goin' on around here right now, but if my girl's involved I am too," Chris taps the budge in her jacket which conceals her weapon.

Mercedes rolls her eyes. "We don't need your help dyke! It's gonna take more than lickin' pussy to get us out of this shit."

Chris takes two steps to her and says, "You know they say women who are afraid of other women's sexuality, have secret tendencies. So what's up, you want me to hit that shit?"

Mercedes walks up to her and steals her in the face. "Bitch you got me fucked up! I'm STRICTLY DICKLY!"

Chris rubs the side of her cheek and says, "You got that but I promise…you WON'T get another one. Now I felt exactly like you did when you called me a dyke. Don't disrespect me and I won't disrespect you. I love Yvette, and if you can't see it, that's your fuckin' problem but I'm not leavin' here wit' out her!"

Mercedes grabs the child's gun off the ground and puts it in the back of her jeans. Then she says, "You know what, it don't even matter to me." She walks away from her and toward the hallway steps. "Cause once Yvette finds out you here, she goin' off anyway. I just hope you ready for it."

"I guess I'ma have to take my chances."

EMERALD CITY SOLDIER
"WE'LL TRY, BUT WE CAN'T MAKE NO PROMISES."

"I think they in one of the last eight apartments on the eastside of the hall," Yvette whispers. "Nassir just texted me and told me he inside one of the apartments wit' one of Black's niggas and he saw the rest going in apartments down there too. Nassir got an orange Northface jacket on so don't hurt him if you see him."

"We got it," somebody says. "We won't hit Nas."

"Cool. Nassir said they know we comin' but they don't know when," Yvette continues to whisper as every one huddles at the west side of the hall. "We goin' in two's and kickin' doors down. If you can help it, try not to hit up no kids."

"We'll try, but we can't make no promises," another soldier says.

"How we splittin' up?" Doctanian asks.

"Everybody grab a man," she says watching them pick partners.

When Kenyetta notices Derrick and Doctanian chose each other she says, "I want you guys to pick somebody else. The plan will work better if we have you two paired up wit' one of the newer soldiers."

"She right," Yvette responds. "So Doc, you take Adriel and Derrick you go wit' Paul. Everybody else can stay where they at."

As they are preparing to move toward the end of the hall, Mercedes and Chris walk up the stairs behind them and into the hallway. Everyone turns around and aims in their direction until they see whom it is.

"Damn, Mercedes! We almost blazed you," Kenyetta says. "What's Chris doin' here?"

"Ya'll go 'head," Yvette responds to everyone to keep her privacy. Everyone walks away except Mercedes and Chris. And her knees grow weak the moment she sees Chris's face.

"What...what you doin' here?" Yvette asks looking at her and Mercedes.

"I told her not to come, Vette, but she wouldn't listen."

"If you here," Chris points at Yvette, "Then so am I. And it don't look like you gotta lotta time to make a decision so we betta move," Chris takes out her glock and cocks it back making sure it was ready to fire.

Chris was right. There was no time to dispute because her men were already on their way to deal with the violators and she needed to be with them too.

"If this is what you want," Yvette says pulling out her weapon. "Then let's hit it." She walks toward her men. "Everybody, move slowly and quietly," she whispers. "Shoot to kill."

As Derrick walks with Paul, Doc notices how Paul looks at Derrick. It's as if he has ill will in his heart towards him.

"You aight, man?" Doctanian asks Paul.

"Wh...why you say that?" he stutters.

"Just checkin'," he responds sizing him up.

"Aight...on two we knockin, down doors," Yvette directs as they all take their positions in front of an apartment.

With her hand in the air, she counts down with her fingers….one…two and on three they kick the doors in.

"Don't move or I'ma shoot!" one soldier yells.

"If a nigga so much as wink I'm burnin' this bitch down!" someone else screams after kicking in a door.

Some men came up empty handed while others locate their marks and fire. Tenants who were uninvolved were running everywhere for cover. They poured out of the doors like water.

"Go to the community center, you'll be safe there!" Yvette tells the people after seeing them run for safety. Chris remains by her side watching her every move to ensure her safety. She wasn't use to seeing Yvette in *boss action* but could tell she was in her element.

When Yvette and Chris kick in another door, they see a lady sitting on the couch with two men on each side of her. All three of them had their eyes glued to the TV and the men's arms were resting on the couch behind her.

"What's goin' on here?" she asks.

"Nothin'," the woman nervously says shaking her head. Her eyes don't leave the television. "Just watching TV with my boyfriend."

"Oh really? Which one?"

A tear streams down the woman's face alerting Yvette instantly. Before she answers, one of them reaches on the side of the couch and fires in their direction. Yvette ducks the bullet that misses her head by inches. Chris drops to the floor and shoots the dude who fired in the kneecap. The other man grabs the lady's head and holds a gun to her temple.

"I'ma shoot this bitch!" he promises standing up with her. "Now I'm gettin' the fuck outta here and ain't shit you goin' do 'bout it."

"We can't let you do that," Yvette tells him. "So you betta let her go."

"Don't fuck wit' me, Yvette! I'll shoot her!"

"I'm sorry," Yvette tells the lady who is shaking nervously, pleading for her life. "But we can't let him leave."

"P...please, Yvette. I...I want to live. Please don't let him kill me."

"If you let us leave I promise I won't kill her. I don't want nothin' to do wit' this no more," he continues with the gun shaking inside his hand. If he shook any harder he'd fire by mistake anyway. "I just wanna go home."

"It's too late for that nigga," Chris says from the floor hitting him in the middle of the head. His body drops and his weight pulls the woman down with him.

Yvette's finger was on the trigger preparing to shoot him herself but Chris beat her to the punch. The woman get's up, looks down at her assailant, and runs screaming out the door.

"Damn," Yvette says looking at the body and then Chris. "You ain't no joke."

"You fuckin' wit' a heavyweight," she winks. "Now let's finish what we started.

They enter the hallway to continue on their mission to kill anyone who didn't belong. They had already lost three men in the war but the violators had lost many more.

When Derrick was about to kick the last door in, Doctanian grows increasingly uneasy with the way Paul is acting. He doesn't trust him and decides to go with his instinct. So the moment Derrick kicks the door in, and Doc sees Paul point the gun to the back of Derrick's head preparing to squeeze the trigger, he walks up behind him and blows his brains out.

"What the fuck," Derrick says moving out the way.

"That nigga was 'bout to kill you, man," Doc says looking down at the lifeless body before him. He smiles and says, "You lucky I'm...," Before he finishes his sentence, he was hit twice in the back by someone behind him.

He was so concerned with Derrick, that he didn't assess his surroundings. Derrick fires multiple times into the man's chest that shot Doc. It wasn't until he hit the floor that he recognizes the man as one of his own. He actually answered to him in Emerald. All this time, the man had larceny in his heart and Derrick never knew. After Derrick makes sure his own life isn't in danger, he bends down and lifts Doc's head.

"Damn, Doc. Why you let 'em catch you, huh?" Derrick continues trying to hold back his tears. Blood oozes out of Doc's body.

Although Doctanian left Emerald city, the two were very close and it hurt him to see him like that. They held secrets about one another no one else knew but them. It was Derrick who Doctanian first chose to tell he killed Dex and Stacey, because Thick blackmailed him. And it was Derrick who prevented Doc from taking his own life. Now Doctanian had repaid him with his life.

"I...I...," Doc's words are gargled by the blood escaping his nose and mouth.

As the other Emerald City soldiers claim victory, they grow silent when they look for Derrick. When they spot him in the doorway holding Doc, Kenyetta, Mercedes, Yvette and Chris walk toward them.

"Fuck!" Yvette yells punching at the wall seeing Doc's body.

Chris grips her and holds her tight as she cries on her shoulder.

"Who got him?" Mercedes asks holding back her tears.

"The nigga lying at your feet," Derrick responds. They look at him.

"Coney? Damn!" Mercedes says.

"Damn, Doc," Kenyetta adds looking at his face. He looks terrified. "I'm sorry we let you come back, man. We shoulda told you to stay away from Emerald. You did good to get away. Fuck!"

Yvette pushes away from Chris and says, "They gonna pay for this shit, Doc. On my life niggas is gonna pay for this shit!" She was taking it the hardest because she was the one who called him.

"We got all of them niggas," Nassir says walking up to Yvette. "Everybody that was wit' Black gone," he glances down and sees Doc. "They hit Doc?" Nobody responds to the obvious.

Doc opens his mouth and grips Derrick's shirt, "I...I...d...de," his words don't exit.

"Don't talk, man."

Doc grips him again and says, "I...deserve...this for k...killin...d...D...Dex and...Stacey. I...I'm...sorry."

"What did he say," Mercedes asks.

Doc takes his last breath and closes his eyes.

"Nothin...," Derrick lies deciding to take his secret to his grave. "It was between us."

The air is immediately filled with remorse and fear that Doc's been murdered. Quiet chatter fills the hallway but Yvette remains silent and walks away from the crowd. She has a moment of clarity and suddenly things being to make sense.

"They were pawns," she says to herself. "They were fuckin' pawns. They were never 'sposed to make it outta here alive."

She knew then that Black sacrificed his own men for the bigger picture. He wanted Emerald to be preoccupied with the men in Unit B, so that they'd overlook what was really happening...a takeover. But the moment the thought enters her mind, Black's real warriors come through their gate, armed and ready for war.

BLACK WATER

OPERATION TAKEOVER

Black Water sits in his Rolls Royce a few blocks down from Emerald. He was speaking to his men on the phone before they rush the gate.

"Aight, this it! Ya'll better go in there and wrap that shit up in an hour, it's 12 now and that's more than enough time. We got the best weapons in DC so your jobs should be easy. If you feel like shit is too rough, remember bitches run this city and then imagine what I'll do to you if shit don't go my way. Make it happen."

Six vans filled to capacity with his crewmembers roll past him. He smiles and says to his driver, "Take me to that strip club off of New York Avenue in D.C."

"The Rouge?" The driver asks in his deep heavy voice.

"Yeah. I wanna see some pussy before I turn into the richest man in the city."

"You got it, boss."

As his driver pulls off, the first van enters Emerald and parks in a location were it could avoid bullets. They were given the layout by their inside man, who are now dead within the walls.

The moment the van parks, the Emerald City members assigned to guard the yard fire at the van with all they have from the windows and the rooftops. The bullets bounce off of the bullet proof vehicle with ease. Covered in bulletproof vests, the men swing the door open and run out. The sixth man remains inside along with the driver. His duty would come later.

Once outside of the van, the men holding M240 machine guns lay into the buildings with extreme firepower. Pieces of bricks from the units fall off the building like clay. Windows shatter and many of the Emerald City men who are on the front side of the building are instantly killed. The bottom line was this...their weapons couldn't be fucked with.

Not expecting to face this type of artillery, most of the Emerald City men banish their post and run for cover, away from the front of the building. When enough damage is done, the sixth man exits the vehicle carrying a bullhorn. Before saying anything, he brushes his suit off with his hand.

"By now you know we not fuckin' around," a tall light skin man says. He looks more like a lawyer than a killer. "The next move is up to you."

Each of Black's men remain in front of the units waiting to fire again if need be. They survey the grounds looking for anything or anyone out of place.

"Black Water is fair...So this is what we gonna do. We gonna give anybody who wants to live a chance to leave," the loudness of the bullhorn echoes throughout Emerald. "I'm gonna count to five, and if you walk out before I count down, we'll let you past without fail. But if you don't leave OUR city, you gonna die. The choice is yours and it will only be given only once. 1...2...3."

When he says three the next five vans enter Emerald City and park in front of each of the units in Emerald. The men already outside holding their machine weapons keep their aim in case someone fires. Once each van parks, the eight men inside each of vans gets out and stand on the steps of each unit.

"I guess no one wants to live," he chuckles. "I'll give you credit for having heart while it still beats. You made a major mistake by not taking Black up on his kind offer. 5!" he continues before getting safely back into the van.

The first group of men holding the weapons unleashes into the side of the buildings while the others jumps out and run inside the units. A full fledge war begins.

EMERALD CITY SQUAD
"WE ALL DROPPED THE BALL ON THIS SHIT."

Yvette and her ten crew members were standing in the hallway in Unit B when they heard…*tat*…*tat*…*tat* multiple times. The sounds followed by light crashing noises resemble rocks falling off of mountains.

"What was that?!" Nassir yells. "Sounds like Mac tens!"

"What the fuck?!" Derrick responds standing up in the hallway, Doc's lifeless body still lying on the floor.

"It sounds like a whole rack of 'em too," was the last thing Nassir says before his head is blown clean off his body.

After Nassir is killed, bullets fly over their heads and against the hallway walls like rain going in the opposite direction. The force of the bullets cause the walls to crumble with extreme ease.

"Run!!!!!!" Yvette screams as they take off toward the far end of the hallway. "Go to the last apartment on the left!"

All of them run for cover while the guns continue to do major damage to the building. When they get to the apartment, they rush inside and the men move a heavy China cabinet placing it in front of the door. The door was already open and no one was inside but them.

"Move to the bedroom in the back! They must be firin' from the field." They do as she says closing the bedroom door behind them. Once inside, everyone sits on the floor.

"What's goin' on?" Mercedes asks out of breath ducking as low as possible. "It sounds like the National Guard out there."

"It's gotta be Black," Yvette responds shaking her head. "I knew this was a set up. What was I thinkin'?!"

"Don't blame yourself, Yvette. We all dropped the ball on this shit," Kenyetta consoles.

"Ya'll must've pissed the wrong nigga off," Chris adds still not believing what was happening. *TAT...TAT...TAT...TAT*, continues to sound off in the background.

"I knew that nigga was plannin' somethin' else," Derrick adds. "I shoulda hit him in Tyland like I planned!"

"Don't beat yourself up, baby. We didn't have time to plan. Everything happened so quickly," Mercedes replies.

"Did ya'll see Nassir's head get blown off," one of the young soldiers asks. He was visibly shaken and in shock. "One minute he was talkin' and the next minute his head was gone."

"Don't think about that," Mercedes tells him. "We have to focus."

"I...I gotta tell ya'll somethin'" Kenyetta says preparing to tell them about Black. "I...'"

"Kenyetta, this don't have nothin' to do wit' you," Mercedes cuts her off. "So leave it alone. Aight?"

Kenyetta is surprised that Mercedes doesn't want her to reveal her secret about dealing with Black, and sneaking him inside. She decides not to speak about it and nods in agreement.

"I'm not tryin' to give 'em Emerald," Yvette says plainly. "I can't give these niggas our home."

And then they hear a voice which says, *"By now you know we not fuckin' around. The next move is up to you."*

After they listen to what the stranger was saying on a bullhorn, fear washes over them.

"You think they really gonna let us go?" the young soldiers says hopefully.

"No...this may be it. I don't care what he says, they never gonna let us leave outta here alive," Yvette advises softly.

"Baby, don't say that shit," Chris tells her. "We gettin' the fuck outta here!"

"Chris, even if me and the girls do walk out, they gonna murder us the moment our feet hit the concrete. They can't let us leave here alive. Trust me. Black knows the only way to keep Emerald if he takes it, is to murder us. Otherwise we comin' back fightin'.."

Kenyetta and Mercedes look at one another and drop their heads.

"Why don't ya'll go 'head," Yvette tells the soldiers and Chris. "We gonna stay. It's us they want not ya'll."

"You lost your fuckin' mind!" Chris tells her.

"Yeah, you must be trippin' if you think I'm leavin' my shawty and ya'll in here alone. If we in it, we in it together!" Derrick tells her.

Silence fills the small room while gun fire gets louder outside the apartment.

"I can't believe its gonna happen like this. I mean...I always knew I'd die in Emerald, but I always thought it would be more peaceful. Like in my sleep or somethin'," Mercedes says looking around at everyone.

"At least you thought about dying," Kenyetta responds. "I figured I'd live forever."

Chris wraps her arm around Yvette and holds her tightly. "If you die at least you're dyin' wit me."

"You really love her don't you?" Mercedes asks.

"Wit' my life," Chris responds looking at Yvette.

"I can feel it," Mercedes says. "I'm so sorry, Chris…for unleashin' on you. And I apologize for the smack."

"You smacked, my baby?" Yvette asks.

"Yeah…she got one out on me. But it's cool though. That shit don't even matter no more."

Mercedes grips Derrick and Kenyetta and Mercedes hold one another. The sounds of machine weapons grow closer.

"They in the building, ya'll. They lookin' for us. They know we here," Mercedes tells them.

"Well I hope they ready for a battle, cause I'm not givin' up easy," Yvette tells them. "I got five bullets, how many ya'll got?"

"Eight…six…ten…two…nine," they say.

"Well…that sounds like enough for a hell of a fight," Yvette assures them.

All of a sudden she starts laughing.

"What's so funny?" Mercedes asks.

"I'm just remembering when you and Derrick use to go at it all the time," she giggles. "I thought ya'll were gonna kill one another. And now ya'll all bunned up and shit."

"I know right," Kenyetta cosigns.

"He use to get on my fuckin' nerves!" Mercedes says looking into his handsome face. "Now I can't live without him."

"I hope so," his tone is soft but the implication of her infidelity looms. "But I never hated you," he continues looking at Mercedes bruised but beautiful face. "I knew from the moment I saw her, that she was the one. Everybody else saw it too that's what was fuckin' me up," he smiles. "You everything to me," he says seriously. "You my soul mate. And if I got any say so in the next life, I'ma choose you again."

There wasn't a dry eye in the room. Yvette stands up and holds out her hand. One by one everyone gets up and places their hands on top of hers.

"Emerald city in life and death," Yvette says.

They repeat after her, "Emerald city in life and death!"

"If I gotta die, I rather die with ya'll. I'm goin' out wit' some real ass niggas," she looks around at them.

"We proud to go out wit' you too," one of the soldiers say.

As they say their goodbyes, Black's men reach their floor with orders to kill them without questions asked.

UNIT C

"IN WAR THERE ARE ALWAYS CASUALTIES."

In Unit C, Black's kids had already killed ten men and had taken control of the stash houses. Because Wallace, Lando and Neo didn't get a chance to relay Mercedes' message about the kids being possibly dangerous, the soldiers' guards were down and they paid with their lives. And now that Black's men had arrived to take the children home, they were free to go, escaping any wrath.

"Everything's clear," one of Black's men, who's holding a machine gun says to the child. He remains in the doorway of the stash house, his foot props it open. "I'm ready to take ya'll downstairs. Get your mother."

As they spoke, men on Black's squad came in and out of the apartment removing drugs and money.

"I'll get her now," Lance, Black's son says. "They ready, ma. We gotta leave. They got the van parked out front."

His brother's push pass him and enters the hallway. They'd had enough excitement for the day and just wanted to go home.

"You ready, ma?" Lance asks his mother who's in a daze.

"I don't wanna leave your brother," Shade says. "Nathan's still in here some where."

"You heard what they said...Auntie Shannon was killed. Nathan might be dead too. We gotta move on, ma. In war there are casualties," he says with conviction.

"Lance, I know. You don't have to tell me that." She says sternly.

"If I ain't gotta tell you, what's up, then?!" the kid shouts. "You actin' like you don't get it. Dad would flip if he saw you actin' like this!"

With the mention of Black she pulls herself together and stands up.

"I'm coming," she walks behind her children to the van.

Her heart was broken because her sister was dead and her child was missing. But she knew she couldn't blame anybody but herself, and that hurt worse. She felt the burning sensation rising in her nose forcing her to cry. But if she showed emotion, Black would certainly punish her in the worst way. Although he reserved violence for the children, he didn't spare his women if they showed signs of weakness during dire situations.

Instead of crying she sat quietly in her seat reciting her son's words, "In war there are causalities."

She added her own words and said, "even if the causality is my own son."

THE COMMUNITY CENTER
"WAKE UP YOUNG MAN. EVERY-BODY GOT GUNS."

The community center is jammed packed with people displaced from their homes in Unit B. Hope was in their hearts that soon, the fiasco would be over and they could return home.

Nathan opens his eyes and realizes he's sitting in a hard plastic orange chair. One of the tenants covered him earlier with her jacket and when he jumps up, he pushes it off. Happy the child was doing better, the tenants smile at him slightly.

"You aight, lil nigga?" Lando asks when they see him standing.

"What happened?" he says although he remembers.

"You shot my man that's what happened. And if you try some shit like that in here, you won't be gettin' back up."

"Why you do that anyway?" Neo questions him.

Nathan thought for a minute about what he was going to say and remembers his conversation with Wallace.

"Cause I was mad," he says pouting.

"Mad about what?"

"I was mad that…that…they killed my aunty," he says sadly. "I wanna go home," he cries. "Please take me home."

"You ain't goin' home no time soon so you might as well get use to it," Neo tells him looking out the window. "None of us leavin' here tonight."

"Where you learn how to shoot anyway?" Lando interrogates.

"My dad taught me."

"Ain't you too young to be holdin' a gun?"

"I guess…but my dad don't think so."

When Lando walks toward the window to look out too, Nathan rushes toward them and removes the gun out the back of Neo's jeans.

"Put your hands up!" he warns.

Neo and Lando turn around throwing their hands up in the air. The sad expression on the child's face is replaced with satisfaction.

"Sorry…but I gotta go," he tells them.

"Son, why don't you put that gun away," one of the elderly men says. "You're gonna hurt somebody or yourself."

"Fuck you," he yells. "What you think I'm playin' or somethin'? I'm not playin' wit' ya'll! I'm leavin'."

"Son…put the gun down," the man begs him. "I don't want to see you hurt."

Scared that the man would tackle him and take the weapon, he shoots him in the shoulder. Everyone gasps in disbelief.

"I coulda killed him," he says moving the barrel of the gun around the room. "I coulda killed him but I didn't. I'm a sure shot. See," he says as he fires into a picture of Stacey and Dex on the community center wall. The bullet went straight into her head. "See, if I wanted to, he'd be dead. All I wanna do is go home. That's it."

"Aight, lil' man," Neo says holding his hands in the air. "You got it."

In the back of the room, a man who'd brought his own weapon sat next to his wife quietly. Not even she knew he was toting.

But when she looks at her husband, and sees the handle in his hand she says, "Don't honey. He's just a child."

Many thoughts ran through the man's mind, including not being able to defend his wife of thirty years. He hated how a disability he gained in the war, forced them to live in the worse conditions...Emerald city, a project. His wife who could barely read and write took odd jobs cleaning homes for rich people in Maryland just to make a little more money than what the government gave them on his disability checks. He felt worthless.

Despising how his life had turned out, and how the young people had taken over Emerald City turning it into an even worse nightmare, he decides to take it out on someone.

"Pete!" his wife screams when he stands up, fires and shoots the child in the chest. His body falls to the floor.

"OH MY GOOOOOOOD!!!" someone cries out. Everyone looks at the man and then the slain kid.

Neo and Lando rush the man taking his weapon. They didn't want him unleashing on them next.

"Sorry old, man," Lando says gaining access to his 9 mili. "But I'ma have to get this up off you."

The man sits back down without a fight. Besides, he did what he wanted, make someone pay for his failures.

"Why, baby? Why?" his wife cries softly. "He was a baby."

"You saw that boy's eyes, Estelle. If he lived, he would've been nothin' but a stone cold killer."

"Who are you? 'Cause I don't know you no more!" she says before getting up to sit at another seat far away from him.

"Thanks, old man," Neo says to him after taking back his weapon from the dead child. "That lil' nigga was crazy anyway. You did everybody a favor. Don't worry, we didn't see nothing. Right everybody?"

No one says a word because they already know the unspoken rule. Keep your silence and keep your life.

"He wasn't the only one crazy you know?" one of the older ladies says. A few people gasp.

"What you talkin' 'bout?" Lando asks.

"I'm talkin' about you. The both of you! All of you Emerald City bangers are just as crazy as that child! Where do you think he got it from?"

"Whateva!" Lando brushes her off.

"Look what ya'll helped them killers do to our homes. Look!" she points with her wrinkled finger toward the door. "We livin' like we're in a foreign country. Locked up and afraid of our own people. You young boys don't give a shit about what you're doing to our generation or your own."

"I'm not tryin' to hear that shit," Neo laughs. "If anything we protectin' you right now cause if we weren't here, who knows what would happen!"

"Wake up young man," another man says. "Everybody got guns. Don't you see?"

"You're destroyin' us," another female tenant adds. "You're destroyin' your own people. You better than this. I know you are."

"Look...in case ya'll didn't fuckin' notice, I'm in here with you. I'm on your side," Neo explains.

"You're selling drugs and killing your own people, you might as well be out there with them. You're on money's side."

The preaching was becoming unbearable to Neo and Lando and they wanted out. If things didn't end soon, they could honestly see themselves killing somebody else.

"Listen…what's done is done! Ain't nobody ever teach me nothin'! I mean, how many of ya'll ever did anything for me besides tell me to get away from your front door? When I was a youngin' comin' up in dis fucked up project, nobody ever did shit for me. I had to go out and make moves to feed my family. And now you wonderin' why we this…and why we that. Take a look around! The blame is just as much yours, as it is ours!" Lando tells them.

"So you blamin' us now," an old lady asks.

"I'm blamin' anybody who blamin' me. You think I wanna be livin' like this? Fuck no! But I'll tell you this, I'm willin' to do what I gotta do and I don't give a fuck who got somethin' to say 'bout it." Lando continues.

"Son…we did our work already," she says to him softly. "It's because of us, you ain't got to do this no more, but you choose to. We marched for civil rights we spoke up for our freedom. You just choose not to take advantage of it. We did what we had to so that you all can have a part of the American dream. So stop blamin' everybody else and start lookin' at yourself."

"You know what…sit your old ass down and shut the fuck up. I'm through talkin' to ya'll." When they didn't sit down quick enough he pulled out the man's weapon and cocked it back. "Do I gotta ask you again?"

Everyone sits down and Lando looks out of the window. What the woman said weighed on him and he was angry. Sure he didn't want to live the lifestyle he was but he didn't see any other alternative.

As he stares out the window, he sees ropes dropping down the walls of Emerald. Then he sees one man after the other sliding down it. There were many men.

"Cut the lights off," Lando yells.

"They in the back now!" Neo warns.

Everyone starts making noise.

"Shut the fuck up before they hear us," Lando tells them. "I'm not fuckin' around!"

Everyone grows as silent as possible. When the lights go out, Neo and Lando continue to peek out of the blinds. They fear Black has stepped up his operation, and was not letting anyone leave Emerald alive. Now the seriousness of the situation had finally set in...for both of them.

DISTRICT OF COLUMBIA POLICE DEPARTMENT

"YOU BETTER BE CAREFUL ABOUT THE SHIT YOU SAY AROUND HERE. YOU JUST MIGHT COME UP MISSIN'."

"What you want to eat, Jones?" Officer Tath says standing over his desk with a pen and a pad. "We're about to put our orders in now.

"I'm not hungry," he responds never looking away from his computer screen.

"We ordering from V-Burgers," Tath persists, hoping he'd change his mind to get the discount on the delivery charges.

"I said I'm not hungry. I didn't come here to eat no expensive ass burgers from V's. I came here to uphold the law but that's not what ya'll wanna do around here." This time he looks at everyone in the station, including Tath.

"What do you mean?" Officer Kerry asks sitting in the desk next to him.

"Stop acting like you don't know what I mean...we've received ten calls in the last hour from people in Emerald city but we do nothing about it! Why?"

"It's just the way it is," Tath responds, walking away. "They got their laws and we got ours."

"Do you hear yourself?" Jones asks.

"No do you hear yourself? You're worryin' about a couple of drug dealing niggers when you should be worryin' about yourself."

Jones was heated because although he was far from a nigger, he was still African American.

"Niggers are people too," Jones replies.

"No...," he chuckles. "They're just *Nigger* people."

"I bet you won't be laughing if I call the mayor's office," he threatens.

The smile is wiped clean off his face.

"You better be careful about the shit you say around here. You just might come up missin'," Kerry advises.

Jones turns around, looks at him and says, "We'll see about that."

LONE SOLDIER

"HE FAILED TO CREATE A BACK UP PLAN."

Black's men grew lax as they enter each unit because the search and destroy mission had dwindled to finding Yvette and the other women. But just when they thought victory was completely won, an army more dangerous than theirs enters from the back of the city.

One of Black's soldiers arrives to the apartment Yvette and her crew is in, his weapon aimed and ready. And then, the sound of weapons firing outside startles him. This was odd because he was given word not too long ago that they won Emerald.

"What the fuck?" he says to himself as he walks away from the apartment, and down the hallway toward the staircase door.

The moment he opens the stairwell door, two men who unload multiple bullets into his body rush him. He drops to the floor, and his body prevents the door from closing. Once he's murdered, the men push open the door and step over him.

The sounds of gunfire rises again outside. A war ensues between Black Water's men and another crew. But because Black's men's' guards are down, Black's men drop one by one. Black made a dangerous mistake. He failed to create a back up plan, and that major error, was going to cause him the war.

BLACK WATER
A FEW HOURS EARLIER
"MANY BITCHES WOULD DIE TO BE IN YOUR SHOES RIGHT NOW."

Although she wasn't a dancer, Black Water was turned on to her apparent attraction to other women. She threw dollar after dollar on the stage as the dancers fought for her attention.

"Excuse me, my boss wants to meet you," Black's driver says interrupting her gaze.

She takes one look at the driver and than at Black who's behind her and says, "What are we in middle school?" she laughs and continues, "If he wants to meet me tell him to meet me himself."

With that she tossed her long black hair and returned her focus back on the women. Five minutes later, Black walks up to her.

"You gonna hang out wit' me at my table?" he asks.

"Who's asking? You are your flunky?"

"Me. And I'm only asking once."

The woman looks him up and down and accepts.

"So what's up," she asks sitting next to him.

"You."

"Me?" she points at herself. "How am I up when you just met me?"

"Cause I know what I like."

"And what's that?"

"For one I fucks wit' chicks wit' that long black hair and shit. You my type...trust me."

She waves him off as if she's uninterested.

"No joke. I found the finest thing in here and she's not on stage."

"Is that right?" she smiles.

He doesn't respond.

"You funny." She continues.

"And you bad as shit! So what's your name?"

"Candy." She confesses.

"Candy, huh? I like that. You gonna be mine before the night is out."

They kept each other's company for the rest of the evening. And when the club closes, he invites her to breakfast.

After enjoying a small meal together, Black instructs his driver to take them to a nearby hotel. He continues to drink excessively believing there was much to celebrate later. After all, by the morning, Emerald City would be his.

Once in the hotel room he asks, "So...w...what were you...you doin' in a strip club?" he plops down on the end of the bed and removes his shoes.

"I guess research, since I'm opening my own spot in Virginia in a few months."

"So you stealin' dancers?" he asks stretching his upper body on the bed, as his feet remain planted on the floor.

"Naw...just checking out my competition," she tells him laying in the bed next to him.

"Do you know who I am?"

"No...who are you?"

"I'm probably the richest nigga you'll ever meet in your life," with that he unbuttons his pants, pulls out his dick and strokes it to a complete thickness.

"Is that right?" she smiles looking at it and then at him. "And how do you know you're the richest man *I've* met in *my* life? I been around money longer than I can remember."

"Cause I run DC and everybody in it," he says as his words began to drag.

"Well I don't live in DC," she says moving closer to him. "But say you are the richest nigga I've ever met...what does that have to do with me?"

"It means for now that I want you to get on your knees, and suck my dick 'cause many bitches would die to be in your shoes right now." There was a brief moment of silence. "Fuck you waitin' on?" he asks with a scowl.

"You use to getting what you want?" Candy says as she stands, walks toward the table and pours two more cups of liquor. "I can respect that." She hands him the plastic cup filled with Remy and sips on the other. "But what you gonna do for me?"

"It depends how good you are," he says downing what was left in the cup before throwing it to the floor. "Now get over here."

"I got you," she responds seductively taking her clothes off. "But let's do it the right way.

◄┄┄┄┄┄┄┄┄┄┄┄┄┄┄┄┄┄┄┄┄┄┄┄┄┄┄┄┄┄┄►

The next morning Black awakes to a throbbing headache from the hotel phone ringing. Candy is next to him naked, with an empty bottle of liquor between them.

"Get up," he says groggily looking around. "We gotta go."

"Already?" she moans. "I was hoping you'd be up for round two."

"Look...get the fuck up or I'm leavin' you here."

"Alright...alright...I'm movin," she says moving around a little before finally getting up.

When they are dressed, they walk toward the limo, Black stumbling the entire way. Candy opens the door and Black slides in, with her right behind him.

"Take me to get some coffee from McDonald's," he tells his driver. "Then take me to Emerald."

When the car doesn't move he asks, "Did you hear me?"

"Yeah...I heard you." Black recognizes the voice despite it not belonging to his driver.

Black sits up straight and leans toward the privacy window separating them. His thick index finger rolls the control window down and the man is revealed.

His own urine escapes his body and he stutters, "Wha...what the fuck is goin' on? W...where's my driver?"

"He gone. But don't worry, I'ma take you where you need to go."

With those words the woman he knew as Candy plunges a knife deeply into his stomach. When his flesh covers the entire blade, she pushes again before twisting it once. Black's mouth opens and he succumbs to the pain.

The driver who is actually Dreyfus, looks at him through the rearview mirror, until his eyes are closed and says, "I told you not to fuck wit', my money. But I ain't gonna have to tell you no more."

EMERALD CITY SQUAD

"LOOKS LIKE YOU ALL FUCKED UP THE CITY PRETTY GOOD."

The sounds of weapons firing ceases completely in Emerald City. And the smell of gunpowder seeps beneath the apartment doors. There was a gloomy presence throughout the city. Death, destruction and fear were all realities.

"I'm goin' out," Yvette says. "I can't stay in here without knowing something."

"You sure we should?" Kenyetta asks. "It's too quiet. That usually means something's up."

"We can't stay in here forever," Yvette warns. "We hid long enough."

"I think she right," Derrick says rising up. The men stood up next to him. "Ya'll follow closely behind me."

The men move the china cabinet and they all walk carefully into the hallway. Pieces of the buildings structure are scattered everywhere. Emerald City is partially destroyed. When they all reach the stairwell, they see a body stuck in the doorway.

"Hold up," Derrick says approaching him cautiously. "Let me check him out." He approaches the body with his 9 drawn. When he reaches the body, he bends down and looks at him. His eyes are wide open so he knows he's dead. "He gone. Let's move on."

Everyone enters the stairwell and runs down the steps to the bottom floor. Pushing the door open and walking outside, their heart's drop at the death and destruction around them. Even the brightness of the sun couldn't soften the despair.

"Damn, boss," one of the men says. "You think they got scared and left?"

"Naw...somethin' else went down," Yvette responds looking around. "I don't know what."

Just when she says that, Black's Rolls Royce enters the gate. Everyone heads back toward the building and remain inside. If he exits the car, they would use every bullet they had to kill him.

"Back up," Yvette says looking through the shattered door. "Cause if that nigga get's out that car, I'm blazin' his ass."

"I'm gettin' in on that too," Kenyetta adds.

When the car drives into the middle of the yard and parks, they remain quiet. And all of a sudden, a woman with silky long hair gets out on the passenger side. Once outside of the car, she removes a long wig and looks up at the units.

"Is that, Carissa?" Yvette asks staring closely through the stained glass door.

"It damn sure look like her," Mercedes adds. "But what is she doin' here?"

Yvette pushes open the building door and everyone follows her. Now they clearly see that it is her.

"Carissa!" Mercedes yells from the top of Unit B.

They run down the stairs and up to her in the middle of the yard. She smiles when she sees their faces and they all embrace without saying a word.

"Oh my God! When I came in and saw the city like this," Carissa says looking around. "I was so worried that something happened to you all. I'm so sorry for abandoning you! Trust me when I say that will never happen again."

"We know...," Kenyetta responds. "And I'm sorry for how I treated you when you wanted to leave. I really am."

"Shut up, bitch! We together now," she says hugging her again.

"But what are you doin' here?" Yvette asks. "And what are you doin' in Black's car?"

Derrick and the soldiers allow the women to have their moment as they keep watch of the city.

"It's a long story so let me make it short. I found out from Lavelle that Black was moving on the city, so I knew we needed help if we wanted to keep what was ours. So I got it."

"Who you get?" Yvette questions.

She walks to the driver side of the car and opens the car. Everyone waits patiently until Dreyfus, who is on the phone, comes into view.

"I'll see you later," he tells the caller. Focusing his attention on the women he says, "Looks like you all fucked up the city pretty good." he looks around.

"You don't know the half," Yvette responds.

"Well look, you got your city back. I'ma get outta here. I gotta flight in six hours to Cancun and I ain't missin' it for anything in the world."

"Thanks, Dreyfus," Yvette smiles. "We'll find some way to repay you."

"Don't worry about it now, you owe me later. Just make sure you pick things up around here and get back to business. And next time, call me sooner."

"Got it," Yvette tells him.

When he drives away Yvette says, "Say what you want, that nigga always comes through when we need him."

"I feel you, but I wonder what he'll want for repayment?" Kenyetta whispers as they look at the car drive out of sight.

"I guess we'll find out," Yvette responds.

"So what happened to Black?" Yvette remembers.

"I spent a dreadful night with him. I even snuck some of that sleeping shit you gave me, Kenyetta. He thought we fucked when we woke up but I ain't touch him. He dead and Dreyfus sending another message that anybody affiliated with Black's business betta get outta Tyland. He's taken it back and he wants us to run it."

"Run Tyland and Emerald?" Kenyetta questions.

"Yeah...think we can do it?" she asks Yvette.

"I'm not sure. To be honest, I'll have to think about it. Somethin' tells me we should focus on home and leave the rest alone."

"I feel you," Carissa responds. "Well...he says if we want it we can have it. And if not, he'll get someone else. They over there right now cleanin' house."

"Hey...what happened to Lavelle?" Mercedes asks.

"Oh...hold on," she smiles. "I have to make another phone call."

LAVELLE

"SO IT'S JUST LIKE THAT, HUH?"

Lavelle sits in a chair next to his bed watching a Katt Williams comedy special on HBO with the two guards. They laugh constantly at his uncensored humor. The more time goes by, the more confident Lavelle grows that he'll make it out of the situation alive. After all, if she'd wanted him dead, he'd be gone already.

When the phone rings, one of the men say, "Lavelle...can you pause that right quick?"

"No problem," he says pausing the show. He knew it was Carissa and he wasn't worried.

"Hey, boss. What's up?"

There's silence as Lavelle sips his Sprite and places it back on the nightstand. As he holds the can, he glances out the window trying to remember all he has to do today. Life seems to move by him and the frustration is quickly becoming irritating. In his heart of hearts all he wants is for Carissa and him to move on with their lives. While looking outside, he smiles at his neighbor who's taking her trash out wearing tight jeans, a white shirt with no bra. But just as quickly as he smiles, it's removed from his face when he sees the raggedy black van drive up and park in his driveway. *"The Vanishers."* He says out loud. He looks at the soldiers who stand up after ending the call with Carissa.

"So it's just like that, huh?" he asks.

"Looks that way, man," one of them says aiming his gun.

"She didn't even wanna speak to me?"

"Naw."

There's a brief knock at the door and one of them leaves the room to open it. Lee returns with another man that Lavelle recognizes.

"Damn...I can't believe it," Lavelle says. "I can't believe I'm dying like this."

"Why? Didn't you say you taught her all she knew?" one of the soldiers asks. Lavelle doesn't respond. "Well...it looks like you did a hell of a job."

A single shot to the head kills him instantly.

CAMERON

"I LOVE YOU AND EVERYTHING I DID WAS SO I COULD BE WITH YOU."

Cameron wakes up with an extreme headache. He rubs his head constantly trying to rid himself of the pain. Moving around a little, he looks around and notices his surroundings. He's in the passenger seat of Toi's 2010 Yukon Denali.

"You aight," she asks him softly. "You don't look too good."

"I…I guess I am. What happened?"

"You got fucked up," she tells him. "You couldn't handle your liquor."

"Well you look okay," he says observing her. "Wasn't you drinking too?"

"Not like you."

When she says that, Cameron feels a pair of hands on his shoulders. He turns around to see who is behind him and cringes at Mercedes' battered face. He reaches for his gun.

"It's not there," Toi says calmly.

"Fuck is going on?" he asks.

"What you think's goin' on?" Yvette responds from the back seat behind Toi.

"Yeah…what you think is up, Cameron?" Kenyetta questions from the third row seat.

"I think he knows what time it is," Carissa adds, she's seated next to Kenyetta.

Cameron swallows hard and looks back at Toi. "Why you do this?"

"Cause I can't stand bitch ass niggas. You shoulda left well enough alone, Cameron. After Mercedes told me the story about Emerald city, I figured if you'd do your children's mother wrong, you'd do worse to me."

"So you would help them kill me?"

"Naw...you did that to yourself."

Cameron laughs a little, and pulls the visor down to look in the mirror at Mercedes.

"Since we bein' real allow me. I don't care about this bitch, Mercedes. I never have. I love you and everything I did was so I could be with you. So tell me...are you really gonna do this to me, baby? What about my Lil' C? He'll hate you for this shit."

"I ain't gonna tell him."

"What about my daughters?"

"It's too late."

"But it doesn't have to be, Mercedes."

"You okay'd some niggas to rape me!"

"I told you I didn't know shit about that! That nigga lied!"

"You didn't stop it either," Yvette adds.

"This between me and Mercedes," he tells her.

"That's where you wrong," Mercedes corrects him. "They have everything to do with this. My friends have been with me every time you broke my heart. All you had to do was keep a promise. That's it. And you couldn't do it. You sold me out twice and there won't be a third."

With that she removes a blade from her pocket and slices his throat open. And just like that, he's gone.

V BURGERS

"LET'S JUST SAY WE USE DC'S FINEST RECIPE."

V Burgers was jumping as usual. The restaurant was jammed pack with police officers and the phone was ringing off the hook with orders. Officers frequented the establishment because during lunchtime, the restaurant gave them free burgers.

"What will it be, sir?" Lee asked.

"Give me two V-Burgers with everything on it," Tath said.

"And what will you have sir?" he asked his partner, Kerry.

"I'll have the same," he smiled rubbing is stomach.

"No problem," Lee said.

"I got to ask you, Lee" Tath started. "What do you all put in your burgers?"

Lee smiled and said, "Let's just say we use DC's finest recipe."

What Lee didn't tell them was that the meat from the burgers came from all the bodies they were paid to remove around the city. The meat was grounded and seasoned to perfection right in the back of their store. And because sometimes the bodies were coming in quicker than they could cook them, the officer's eat free promotion helped clean up their tracks greatly. So little did the officer's know, they were helping keep the streets clean after all...one body at a time.

EPILOGUE

A YEAR LATER

Weeks after the war, the mayor had a full investigation because Officer Jones made a big deal about Emerald City receiving special treatment and being immune from the law. But when the detectives visited, they turned a blind eye to almost everything. After all, Emerald city had many officers on payroll...the detectives included.

Shortly after the investigation concluded that nothing was out of order, Officer Jones was mysteriously transferred out of the precinct and to another department. And after a few complaints from people he arrested, he was later fired. He knew it had everything to do with him breaking silence, but he couldn't prove it.

Emerald city was up and running after a year. It wasn't easy getting order and the women ended up putting millions into Emerald City just to make it safer and stronger than ever. The guard's station was now further inside Emerald, and the gate leading into the property was further out. This way the guard could see on the closed circuit television who was entering before making a decision to open the gate. Security cameras were placed everywhere and each building had a guard who worked for Emerald. Although the DC Government owned Emerald City, it was the squad who made the rules.

Mercedes married Derrick and they lived happily in their home. Both of them were still very active in Emerald and she never stepped out of her relationship again. What she didn't know was that Derrick slept with a girl who lived in Virginia from time to time who was catching feelings for him. Although he forgave Mercedes and would never leave her, he never forgot what he heard Mercedes say she did with Cameron. That changed his commitment to her but not his love.

Lil' C spent a lot of time in Emerald and he was learning the ropes personally from his mother. All he thought about was money and he trusted no one but his mother.

Yvette and Chris lived together and Yvette was working hard to make the relationship successful. The only problem was, they argued constantly. Although they didn't always see eye to eye, their love for one another kept them together.

Carissa became bold with her sexuality and had sex with who she wanted without regard for how they felt. She'd become cold to the idea of love, but open to life. She sold the home she shared with Lavelle and purchased a five million dollar yacht which she kept docked in Southwest DC. She lived there when she wasn't in Emerald.

Six months after the war in Emerald, Kenyetta sold her home. Realizing she didn't want to be alone, she took Carissa's offer to move on her yacht. Just like Carissa, Kenyetta had become turned off to love. When they weren't in Emerald the two of them took trips around the world and were known as heartbreakers. It didn't bother them because at least they were happy and their feelings were guarded.

In Emerald city the fort was stronger than ever and they opened a few legal operations to hide the money they had flowing. Life was good but the war left a lot of wounds. Although they appeared strong on the surface, a thought never left their minds. Can something as disastrous as that ever happen again?

PITBULLS IN A SKIRT 3
BEWARE OF THE BLACK WATER CLAN

EXCERPT

Tamir, one of Black Water's oldest sons was on top of his newest girlfriend. They had just finishing having sex and he was ready for another round. Trey Songz, *Wonder Woman,* song played on the radio.

"What's wrong, sweetheart?" he asked as he gently pushed his manhood toward her love box without entering. He was growing hard again. "You seem like you got somethin' on your mind."

It was hard for her to look at Tamir directly in the eyes because his handsome features made her weak. It was almost as if she was unworthy of him.

"I wanna know if you love me or not."

"You know I do," he said as he slid into her easily. Her mouth opened and he suckled her bottom lip.

"Than...than...why don't you come around as much?"

"Because you not willin' to be the woman I need you to be. You force me to hang out more with my other girls."

"But why do you have to have other girls, Tamir? How come I'm not good enough for you?"

"Cause I'm a man who has needs to be fulfilled. But don't I take care of you? Don't you have every purse and every shoe you desire?"

"Yeeeeeessss," she moaned as his strokes became stronger. "But I don't want you to have other girls."

"That'll never happen, I gotta be honest. Most niggas would just cheat and not tell you about it but that ain't my style. Now, if you can't deal wit' what I need," he said as he opened her legs wider and pushed deeper inside of her. "Than that'll be your choice. I'll just let you go."

"I...don't want you to do that," she cried because making love to him felt surreal.

"Tell me you'll do anything for me," he whispered in her ear.

"I'll...I'll do anything for you."

"You gonna have my baby?"

He'd asked her before but in the past she said no fearing what her mother would do to her.

"I'm scared," she cried.

"You know what," he said pulling out of her. "I'm not fuckin' wit' you no more. When you know what you want, come see me."

Taska didn't get along with her mother, but he was the only boy who could come over anytime he wanted because he paid her mother off. So if Tamir left, all that would end and she'd be lonely.

"Please...don't leave," she stopped him pulling him back on her. "I wanna have your baby."

As she said that, he entered her body again and quickly released his semen into her. Twenty one year old Tamir was just like his father in all senses. He had dreams of growing the Black Water clan just like his father had planned. With his father's children, wives, and grandchildren, the Black Water Clan were already over a hundred deep.

But Tamir was unlike his father in one way. The semen he used to breed was infected with HIV. When he was diagnosed a year earlier, he chose to ignore the doctor's orders to inform his sexual partners. Tamir already had five babies and with the one he was making now, he'd have six.

Breeding was just a part of Tamir's plan. He was saving enough money to leave Virginia, the place his family moved to after Dreyfus put them out of Tyland. He was going back to Emerald to seek revenge for his father's murder, and to finally claim the city his father wanted before he died.

No one told him, it was easier said than done.

PITBULLS IN A SKIRT 2

The Cartel Publications Book Club Discussion Sheet

MAJOR SPOILER DON'T READ UNLESS YOU'VE FINISHED THE BOOK

1. Do you think Mercedes was justified in killing Cameron?
2. Do you think Cameron was in love with Mercedes?
3. Are you angry with Kenyetta for bringing Black on the grounds?
4. Was Carissa wrong for leaving her friends during the worse time in Emerald City's history.
5. What direction do you think Lil' C is going to take in life?
6. Do you consider Mercedes a bad mother for teaching Lil' C the drug life?
7. Do you think the women are irresponsible for running and operating a million dollar drug operation?
8. Which character do you relate to?
9. If you could earn money by running a drug operation, would you?
10. What are the consequences of living the drug lifestyle?

The women could've done so many things to prevent their fate. And although this is a fiction story, it's amazing how characterizations relate to real life. Think thoroughly about your current situation and make decisions before making moves. You'll be surprised at how much time you'd save yourself and how better your life would be.

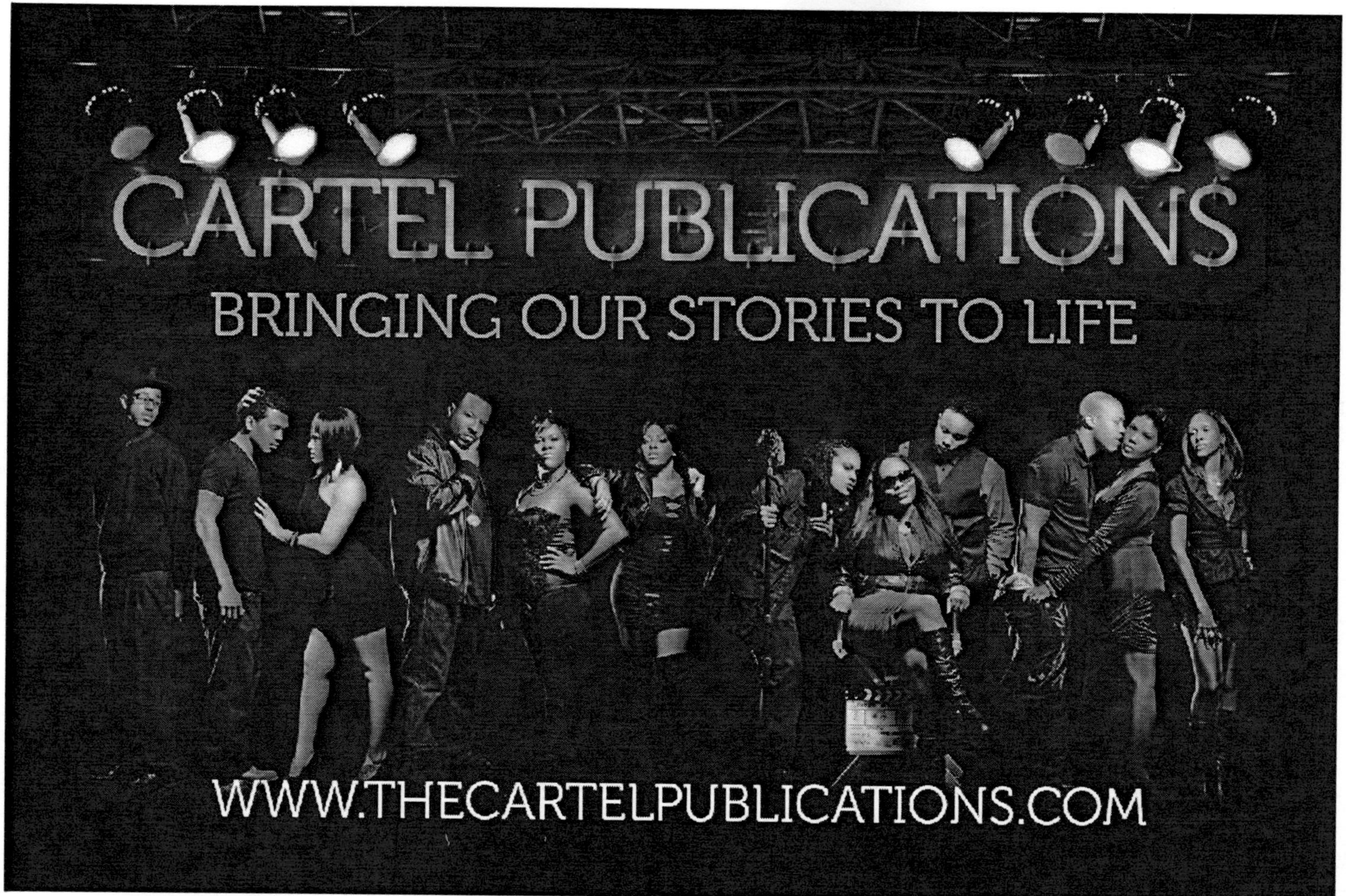
CARTEL PUBLICATIONS
BRINGING OUR STORIES TO LIFE
WWW.THECARTELPUBLICATIONS.COM

CARTEL PUBLICATIONS
PRESENTS

The Cartel Collection
Established in January 2008
We're growing stronger by the month!!!
www.thecartelpublications.com

Cartel Publications Order Form
Inmates ONLY get novels for $10.00 per book!

Titles		_Fee_
Shyt List	_____	$15.00
Shyt List 2	_____	$15.00
Pitbulls In A Skirt	_____	$15.00
Pitbulls In A Skirt 2	_____	$15.00
Pitbulls In A Skirt 3	_____	$15.00
Victoria's Secret	_____	$15.00
Poison	_____	$15.00
Poison 2	_____	$15.00
Hell Razor Honeys	_____	$15.00
Hell Razor Honeys 2	_____	$15.00
A Hustler's Son 2	_____	$15.00
Black And Ugly As Ever	_____	$15.00
Year of The Crack Mom	_____	$15.00
The Face That Launched a Thousand Bullets		
	_____	$15.00
The Unusual Suspects	_____	$15.00
Miss Wayne & The Queens of DC		
	_____	$15.00
Year of The Crack Mom	_____	$15.00
Familia Divided	_____	$15.00
Shyt List III	_____	$15.00
Raunchy	_____	$15.00
Reversed	_____	$15.00

Please add $4.00 per book for shipping and handling.
The Cartel Publications * P.O. Box 486 * Owings Mills * MD * 21117

Name: _____

Address: _____

City/State: _____

Contact # & Email: _____

Please allow 5-7 business days for delivery. The Cartel is not
responsible for prison orders rejected.

CPSIA information can be obtained
at www.ICGtesting.com
Printed in the USA
LVOW12s1452060516

487046LV00001B/162/P